Stock Car Sam

Charlie Loomis

ISBN: 1453704132
ISBN-13: 9781453704134

On the web at www.cloomis.com
Printed By createspace.com

ACKNOWLEDGEMENTS

For superb technical advice:

Ted Marsh and crew at Marsh Racing, Old Lyme, Connecticut.

Dave Bayes, owner/driver of #3 and his wife Pam, Hillside Auto Repair, Vail Mills, New York.

For Encouragement and Support:

All who read my first book, Motocross Mike, and wanted more.

My children Jeff, Kim and Val.

My wonderful grandkids who love Grandpas's writing.

Jami Carpenter, a splendid and much appreciated editor.

Judi Moreo, a kindly and excellent motivational influence in my life.

Jim Brosch for the great cover art.

Above all, my wonderful and supportive wife, Ginny, who never complained when I rolled out of bed at 3:30 in the morning to capture one of my brainstorms.

DEDICATION

For John Marsden Gurga - a young man who showed us all the true meaning of courage. John is recovering from burns over eighty percent of his body suffered from an unfortunate camping accident.

AUTHOR'S NOTE

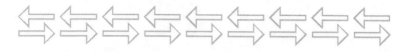

This book is in recognition of the young women who are making tremendous inroads in the field of motorsports. Women are proving that they can seriously and successfully compete in a field formerly dominated by men. Women are finding new career paths in all phases of motorsports from dirt bikes to motorcycle drag racers and from jalopy racing on local dirt tracks to the sophisticated Indy cars of today. On any weekend they can be found racing around local tracks at sixty miles an hour or over two hundred miles an hour on tracks like the Indianapolis Speedway. We are grateful for their spirit and dedication as they break new ground for future young women everywhere.

CHAPTER ONE

The noise sounded horrible to Samantha. She felt the whole car shake and rattle from the violent thumps and bangs as it collided with another car. It was not her fault, but then, maybe it was; sometimes in stock car racing, crashes happen so fast that you are never quite sure what is happening or who caused them.

She had been trying to pass another car: number twelve. She knew it was Chuck Turner, her boyfriend, as soon as she got close enough to read the number. Both started racing at age sixteen in the jalopy class; "Run What Ya Brung," they called it. There were some rules, but not many. You did have to install a roll cage and remove the upholstery, take out the windows and replace the windshield with heavy wire mesh — to protect the driver from flying rocks and debris thrown up by cars ahead of them on the dirt tracks — but the rest was pure street stock, no changes allowed.

She knew she would get by Chuck eventually as he was becoming more and more out of control in the corners, trying hard to stay ahead of Sam. Sam was pushing him, right on Chuck's tail at every turn and straightaway, and she could tell Chuck was getting nervous. She had to pass Chuck to get to the three leaders in front of him.

She was finally passing him on the outside, but just as she was, Chuck lost it and slid up into her. Sam thought she was going into the wall and braced for it. She twisted the wheel and crunched down on the throttle to get away from the wall and Chuck, but the nose of Chuck's car was already into her left side. She could feel her car begin to tip on its side. "Oh no," she thought, "I'm going over." And she did — with Chuck right on top of her. Then miraculously he slid off Sam's car and skidded into the infield with hardly any damage.

Suddenly, Sam was upside down in the middle of the track with ten closely-packed cars bearing down on her. The drivers tried to get around her, but there was little room to maneuver and she was hit again and again, the cars spinning her around like a top. Finally, the car came to rest. And then it was over.

She was dizzy and disoriented. She couldn't tell up from down or left from right. Like any driver, she worried about fire, even with advanced fuel cell technology. Forgetting the car was upside down; she quickly unbuckled her seatbelt and fell out of her seat onto her head, twisting her neck enough to make her cry out.

Good thing I've got a helmet on, she thought.

Immediately, safety crews were helping her out of the car. Surprisingly, the worst injury she got was a sprained neck, bruised elbows, and skinned knees, but she was okay. She stood blinking in the harsh lights of the track, a little dazed, but her condition slowly improved as the medics examined her and declared her not seriously injured. She shook her head and removed her helmet and her long, dark hair fell around her face. The bees she imagined swarming around her head gradually went away as she realized her car had been raced for the last time. Even in her dazed state she could tell it probably wasn't worth fixing.

Dave Wright, Sam's mechanic and an employee at her father's auto shop, came running. "You okay?"

Sam nodded; "I think so."

"Wow, that was some crash." He studied her face. "You look out of it.

"I think I am a little. I fell on my head when I unbuckled my seat belt. That was the worst part of the whole deal." She shook her head again and resumed looking over the car.

It was a good thing it was the last race of the season; her car was a mess. It would need a lot of work if it turned out to be salvageable. Something had let loose in the rear end, the radiator was leaking seriously, and the body seemed to be wrenched loose from the frame. The beautiful, custom fiberglass nose that she had saved to buy was destroyed and the front wheels were crooked, indicating some serious frame damage there. *Probably need a new frame*, she thought. But being the last race of the season she would have the whole winter to work on it and she looked forward to it. *If it can be fixed, I'll just take my time and do it right*, she promised herself.

Track services hooked up the car and towed it back to the pits as she and Dave walked back to her pit slot. "Glad it's the end of the season," Sam said.

◦◦

Sam had avoided accidents all season long, but this one had sucked her in. She should have known better than to try to pass Chuck Turner on the outside. His car was a great car, but terrible in the turns and she knew that from prior experiences, racing against him many times. She was even more upset at her poor judgment. "I should have known, Dave," she moaned.

She and Dave got the car on the trailer after a struggle and some help from a crew pit nearby. They toggled the blue and yellow number three tightly to the trailer. The car had started the season with a beautiful paint job that she had lovingly applied and waxed and polished herself. So many had admired it then. Now it was scratched, dented, and twisted into an ugly heap. Still, the car had served Sam well and she hated to junk it. She thought about the track championships the car had won year after year and she heaved a great, sad sigh.

"Buck up, kid," Dave said, "we can build a better one this winter."

Sam Taylor surprised many people. She was small in stature — petite many would say. She was very pretty with long black hair and large green eyes. No one would guess that she was an auto mechanic and an excellent one at that. She did practically all of the body work herself, having learned her trade well in her father's garage. Working with him from a very young age, she decided then to become a race car driver and build and maintain her own cars. This she did.

Dave and Sam had been friends and coworkers on her racecars for a long time. Dave was an excellent engine man and could tune the most cantankerous engine so it ran as smooth as a Swiss watch. He had come to work at Taylor's at Sam's urging. "Please, Dad, he knows racecars and can help me as well as work in the shop. All my friends at the track tell me he's an excellent mechanic. He's got great references. Please hire him."

Jim Taylor was a pushover for his beautiful daughter's demands. Now Dave was Sam's constant companion in the shop and at the races.

"Come on, kid, let's go find your friends," Dave urged gently. He could see that she was sad. They had won the class championship, but the car had probably seen its last race.

They trudged over to the stands to watch the rest of the races with old friends who were there as spectators.

"Hey, Sam, you okay?" they asked.

"Yeah, I'm alright," she said with a shrug of her shoulders. "My car isn't so great, though."

"We noticed. You crashed right here in front of us and we were hoping you didn't get hurt," one said. "Jeez, you were spinning like a top out there."

"If you think it looked bad, you should have been inside. I didn't know where I was."

They all looked up to see Chuck approaching.

"Uh oh; you're in big trouble, Chuck. Put your girlfriend out of the race? Nice work."

Chuck grinned sheepishly. "Well, I didn't do it on purpose."

Sam looked at him, her green eyes blazing. "When are you going to fix that thing so it will turn a corner without taking everyone near you out of the race?" She moved over to make room for him on the bench.

"Sorry I hit you," he said with downcast eyes, "I'm just so busy at work that I don't have much time to work on the car."

Sam looked at him with her best pretend angry look. "Well, you better fix it pretty soon or someone is going to wring your neck and I think I'm going to start doing that right now."

Sam reached for Chuck's neck with both hands, but he ducked away. Chuck knew his girlfriend was small but powerful. She had strong arms and hands from working on cars in her father's shop and wrestling race cars around the local track at the Fonda Fairgrounds.

She and Chuck had been sweethearts since high school. He knew that she would never hurt him on purpose but some of their play wrestling bouts ended up with him having some sore spots on his six foot two inch frame. She ended up tousling his longish blonde hair and giving him a punch on his shoulder.

Chuck swatted her hands away and they ended up in fits of giggles. "At least I didn't put you out at the beginning of the season," he said.

"Yeah, only because most of the time I was ahead of you and didn't have to pass you," she countered. "And I never passed you in the corners. That was my big mistake tonight. I was too eager to get to the lead cars."

They all laughed and turned to watch the next races.

Sam's mind wasn't on the racing, however, so she kissed Chuck on the cheek. "Gotta go; I'm tired and need some sleep. See you at our house tomorrow for dinner?"

Chuck smiled. "You bet," he said. "But I can only stay for dinner and then I've got to drive to North Carolina. Dad and I are bidding on a truck line down there. We're expanding south and we found what looks like a great deal."

She and Dave said goodbye to everyone and left early. They jumped in the truck, already attached to the trailer, and headed home.

It was a quiet ride as both Dave and Sam thought about the day. Each felt some responsibility for the accident. Dave probably should have tweaked the engine a bit more so Sam could power her way out of trouble. Instead, he had decided that a little less horsepower would make the engine last longer and run better in the longer races.

Sam thought she should have had enough foresight to get out of the jam and stay away from Chuck's squirrelly car. Next year it would be different. "Every time I have an accident I learn a little bit more about how to avoid the next one," Sam said. "Experience is the best teacher. I won't let that happen again. Great way to end the season, eh, Dave?"

"Yeah, Sam, but you know if this had happened earlier we probably would have missed a few races — if the car could've even been repaired. If we had to build a new one, we probably would have missed the whole season. You planned it just right."

Sam smiled. "Yeah, great planning, but I didn't intend to smash up the car."

"Besides," Dave continued, "that was a great battle you and Chuck were having. You probably didn't know it, but you two had all the fans out of their seats screaming their heads off. Cool!"

Sam smiled. She could picture the scene. "Dave," she said, "next year we're going to do it better."

"Hey, we got the track championship for street stock again; nothing wrong with that, but yeah, we can always do some things better." Dave nodded his head as they made their way home in the chilly fall air.

Sam didn't have much time during the week after the crash, but on Saturday the shop closed early so Sam was able to look over the car. Dave joined her. "Wow, it looks worse than it did last week," he commented.

"You know with all the work to do on that heap maybe I should just forget about it and move up to pro stock. It's what I want to do anyway. We'll just do it a year earlier. I've got that chassis Bill Wilson gave me when he retired.

He always wanted me to run pro stock with him and said he'd teach me all the stuff I needed to know to run that class. Maybe Chuck will want to join us if he has time to convert his car. He's talked about moving up to pro stock, too. Maybe now's the time."

"Sounds good, but Chuck says he's awfully busy with that growing trucking business of his. Maybe we can give him a hand with his car when we finish ours."

Sam thought about it. "Yeah," she said.

Dave had an idea. "You know the front clip on Wilson's car is pretty beat up from that accident he had in his last race. We can use the one off that old Camaro out back and tack it on to Wilson's chassis. Other than that, the Wilson chassis looks like it's in great shape, since he hadn't had it long before the crash."

Sam shook her head, remembering. She had seen the accident. "That was a real bell ringer. When he dropped off the chassis he told me he had headaches for about three weeks after that crash and that's what made him decide to retire — that and his wife worrying about him at every race."

Dave thought a minute. "I think the engine in your street stock is okay. Maybe we can hoist it out of there and take it over to Jack's Speed Shop and see what he thinks about beefing it up to run in the pro stock class. That engine always ran strong and maybe it will work for us."

"Worth a try," Sam agreed. "When do you want to hoist it?"

"You got time this afternoon?" Dave asked.

"Sure; shouldn't take long."

The two friends worked together and had the engine out of Sam's wrecked car in about an hour. They lowered the engine into the back of Sam's pickup.

"I'll call Jack on Monday to see when I can bring it over," Sam said.

Dave agreed. "Jack will probably be happy to have the engine to work on this winter instead of waiting until next spring."

Sam thought a moment and then said, "I think I'll cut the front clip off the Camaro and tack it on to Wilson's frame this afternoon. I've got some time."

They moved Sam's old beat up street stock out to the boneyard behind the shop and hauled the Camaro in.

"As soon as I get the front clip done, I'll have to do the wheels first on Wilson's chassis so we can roll her in and out if we get busy. I want to keep Dad happy and if we plug up a stall with a stock car he won't be. Got to keep the boss smiling, you know?"

Dave chuckled. "You've got that right," he said. I've got to get home to run a few errands. You don't need me now, do you?"

Sam looked at her friend. "Nope, I'm okay now. I'm just going to do that front clip and tinker with the old car, pull out the gauges, seat, and fuel cell. No sense having them lie around in the snow all winter long."

"Good enough, Sam, I'll see you Monday."

"Thanks for your help, Dave."

Dave jumped in his car and tooted his horn.

"No problem," he called out the open window as he drove away.

Sam waved and turned back to her work.

The Camaro had two flats so she repaired them. The car had set outside for a couple of years and the lug nuts were so rusted she needed an impact wrench to get them off. Then she turned to unhooking all the wires and shafts from the engine in preparation for hauling it out so she could detach the front clip. The engine would be stored, cleaned of the grease and dirt caked on it, and maybe fixed up and used for a spare if she ever needed it.

She knew the Camaro engine was not in great shape but could be repaired. That's why it was in the boneyard. She had bought the car cheap and knew that some of the spare parts might come in handy. Before she could ever use the engine Jack would have to go through it to see if it was salvageable.

As she worked she thought about Chuck and the possibilities of racing with him next year. She knew he was excited about growing his business. They had discussed how much time would be required and if he would even have time to race. She also knew he would be very disappointed if he couldn't race. He loved it as much as she did.

But business called. The new truck line he and his dad were looking at would expand their business deep into the south and would hook up nicely with their whole operation. Chuck would be required to travel frequently until they had it set up to their liking. He hated to miss racing but more than that he hated being far away from Sam for long periods. He knew he would just have to deal with it.

Most Sundays when Chuck was home, he had dinner with Sam at her parents. Her family enjoyed each other's company and Mary was happy to cook for her daughter. Sam had a full kitchen in her apartment but liked her mother's cooking best. Occasionally, she would invite her parents to her place for a simple dish that she loved and loved to make — macaroni and cheese. Her mac and cheese didn't come from a box; she made it from scratch and it was delicious.

After dinner, the two of them would go to Sam's apartment. They'd watch whatever races were being broadcast or DVDs of their own past races or NASCAR races from the video store or Netflix. They loved to watch racing of all types — sports cars, street stock cars, Indy cars, motorcycles, you name it. If they raced, they would watch it.

The Sunday after Sam's big crash, they walked to Sam's apartment after dinner and discussed plans for the following year.

"Boy, your mother can sure cook. That was the best pot roast I ever ate."

"Yeah, she's a great cook. I have to watch myself when I eat with them or I'll blow up like a balloon."

Chuck laughed, "Oh yeah, that one hundred and ten pounds you carry will just grow and grow."

"Hey, remember I told you I was thinking about running pro stock next year?"

Chuck nodded his head. "Yeah, I remember."

"Well, Dave and I decided to go for it. As long as I have to rebuild another car anyway, we might as well make the switch. I just want to continue to move up the ladder. I need more competition. You want to join us?"

"Sounds good to me, but I'm awfully busy. If the deal goes through, I'll be even busier and away from home a lot. No time to race."

She put her arm around Chuck. "Aww, don't say that. I don't want you to leave me anymore than you really have to."

"Well, I'll have to go back to North Carolina to close the deal and take inventory and all that stuff. Dad will help but he doesn't want to go down there alone. After all the arrangements are done, I won't have to go down there so much. They have a real good manager and we're hoping to put him on our payroll. He'll take care of things for us."

"How about if Dave and I help you out after we get ours built?"

"I like that idea, but when will you guys have time to do that?"

"We'll have some nights and weekends when mine is finished."

"If you do that, I want to pay you and Dave. I don't want you to do it for nothing."

Sam smiled, "We'll work something out; don't worry about it. I want you in the same races I'm in so I can continue to whip your butt."

Chuck laughed, "I knew there was a hidden agenda somewhere. Okay, I'm fine with that if you and Dave can work it out."

❦

On another one of those Sundays, she and Chuck were cuddling on her couch. He said to her, "If we ever have kids, do you wonder what they'll look like?"

Sam jumped to her feet, turned to Chuck, pointed her finger at him and said, "Please don't talk to me about having kids or about marriage or anything like that. You know what my goal is. I want to be a NASCAR driver and race Cup cars. That's my only goal right now. I can't be thinking about anything else. I don't know for sure how I'm going to do it, but I sure am going to try and I don't want anything to stand in my way."

Chuck held his hands up palms toward her and laughed. He had never seen her quite so agitated. "Okay, Okay. Gee whiz, I was only thinking out loud."

"Well, don't," she said. "Keep those thoughts to yourself."

"I'm sorry; I guess I never realized how strongly you felt about racing NASCAR. Come on; sit back down."

She sat and he put his arm around her shoulders, pulling her close. He kissed her and buried his face in her long black hair and whispered in her ear, "I love you, and I don't like to see you angry. I'll help you reach your goal any way I can. You can count on that."

She settled down and moved as close to him as she could. She loved the comfort he gave her. "Hey," she said. "I'll take care of you and you take care of me and let's leave it like that. Okay?"

"Yummy," he murmured, his face still buried in her sweet-smelling hair. "I can sure live with that. No problem."

They both laughed and settled in to watch the race on TV.

CHAPTER TWO

The snow was deep and the winter was cold, a record breaker as the thermometer dipped low and the accumulated snow piled higher and higher.

Sam missed the summer weather, but she was also a skier, so she didn't mind winter that much. There was a friendly, family ski area nearby where she usually went on Sundays and sometimes Saturday afternoons if the snow conditions were good.

She loved the Adirondack Mountains and the Royal Mountain Ski Area was only twenty miles away. Often Chuck would go with her, but if he was busy she would go alone knowing she could always find a friend or two to ski with at the mountain. Jim Blaise, the owner of Royal, was a good friend of Sam and her family and was one of her sponsors, so Sam was glad to support the skiing there.

She was also a member of the local health club and worked out there during the week after the shop closed. She had a daily regimen of working out on machine weights after a half-hour session on the treadmill and was among the fittest drivers in the spring when the racing season began. Long races suited her just fine.

But no matter what she did in the winter, the summer and racing was always on her mind.

Sam and Dave spent the winter building Sam's new pro stock racer for the coming season. They carefully measured and installed Sam's custom seat in the new car. They carefully transferred the fuel cell to the Wilson chassis. All the gauges and controls were installed in the custom dash that Sam welded together. Along with everything else, she was also an accomplished welder and could paint a new finish on a car as good as anyone. All firewalls had been constructed according to the rulebook and the car was starting to look like a real cool racer.

They took pride in the way the car looked as well as how it ran, so they replaced most of the body panels. They wanted the car to show well in the pre-race exhibitions at local shopping malls. The car, after all, was a rolling billboard for the family's repair shop, "Taylor's Complete Auto Repairs." They also wanted it to look good for their other sponsors. They were almost ready to roll. All they lacked was a paint job and the engine, which was done and waiting for them at Jack's Speed Shop.

Painting was left until last so Sam could be sure that she could make all the sponsors happy with the placement of their ads on the car. Most prominent, of course, was the ad for "Taylor's Complete Auto Repair."

They tried to fulfill their promise to Chuck to help him turn his street stock car into a pro stock competitor. On his car, however, they fell way behind and found at the end of the winter that they could not finish it. Chuck said not to worry as the southern addition to the trucking business had come about as planned and he found himself very busy. So busy, in fact, that he told them he probably wouldn't have time to drive it anyway, even if it was finished.

Gradually the snow began to melt as the sun moved higher in the sky. Brooks that were tiny streams in the summer were now overflowing with water from melting snow that flowed down ever closer to the sea.

∽

One morning after the long, cold winter, Sam awoke early to a beautiful spring Saturday morning. The air, while still chilly, smelled fresh and clean and the sun was coming up into a clear sky. Sam stepped out of her apartment over the shop and onto the deck she and her father had built the year before. She had pestered her father to put the apartment over the garage and finally her Dad had agreed. They both loved to do carpentry and spent many hours together building a place that Sam could call her own. Chuck helped out, too, when he wasn't tied up at the trucking firm he and his dad ran.

She took a deep breath and smiled. Ah, almost time to go racing. Next week was the first big car show. The following weekend they would have the first chance of the season to run the track in what was called a warm-up session. Sam wasn't worried. She would be ready. The car was very near completion. The engine would go in this afternoon and the new paint job would be done Monday or Tuesday.

She bounded down the stairs from her deck, looking forward to one of her mother's great breakfasts.

The lot where Sam and her family lived was huge and contained all the buildings the family needed. The auto repair business and the house her parents lived in were side by side facing the street. Behind the shop was a parking lot, which they used to store vehicles waiting for repair and also sold some used cars from there as well. It was a little messy but they hid the real messy part behind a big board fence. Dad wanted all racecar parts outside so they had more room for business. Sam hid all her canvas-covered racing spare parts and old engines there. Behind the house, Sam's mom enjoyed gardening and maintained a neat flower garden and lawn. It was the site for many family picnics with friends when the weather was right.

"Morning, Mom," she said as she kissed her cheek.

"Good morning, Sam." She turned her cheek to her to receive her kiss. "Did you sleep well?"

"Sure did, Mom. Morning, Dad; what's on the agenda for today?" She patted her father's shoulder as she walked by.

"Not too much, Sam. We've got a couple of brake jobs and a couple of mufflers to install. We might take on some more work for next week but that's about it. If everything goes okay, you can quit a little early to work on your car. We'll see. How's it going? I've been so busy I haven't had time to look it over."

"It's going really well, Dad. Dave and I'll put the new engine in this afternoon and I'll paint it next week. The car show at the mall is next Saturday and Sunday. I can't wait to get it on the track. It should be fun — big horsepower boost. I hope I can handle it. Pro stock is the way to go," she said as she rubbed her hands together over the plate of pancakes her mother placed in front of her.

❦

That afternoon in the shop her father called out, "Sam, are you working on the brakes on Mrs. Clements car?" He had heard the sound of tools against metal but couldn't be sure where the metal was — on Sam's new racecar or Mrs. Clements brakes.

"No, Dad," Sam yelled back, "but I can do those in no time at all."

"Sam, please take some "no time at all" and get those brakes done before Mrs. Clements gets here. She's a good customer and I don't want to keep her waiting. You can work on your car later. We have to make some money. Business comes first."

"Okay, Dad. I'll get right on it."

To Sam, a beautiful day like today was made only for racing or working on her new racecar. She was glad she had decided to go into the pro stock class. She was tired of the rough and tumble of the street stock class and just wanted to go faster with more skilled drivers.

It was costing what to her was a ton of money — $4000.00 — to have Jack's Speed Shop rebuild the engine. The chassis that Wilson had given her was a lifesaver, in both time and money.

It was now time to design the artwork that she would put on it. She also had to work in her sponsors' names to give them good exposure. Her father paid her to display the shop name on the doors and she had already planned the lettering for that.

At 10:00 a.m. she opened the garage doors and let in the fresh spring air. She took a deep breath and it felt good. Racing was on her mind.

Jim chuckled as he thought about his daughter's love of car racing. "That kid would spend all her time working on that car if she could," he had told his wife the night before. "I never saw anyone who loves racing as much as that kid does."

Mary agreed. "I know, Jim; I used to worry about it, but she is such a wonderful daughter. Why not let her do all she wants to with racing as long as she doesn't get hurt or cost us a lot of money? I stopped worrying about her getting hurt a long time ago. She really is tough and is an excellent driver."

"Yeah," Jim replied, "I don't mind sponsoring her, and it's good advertising. She's using her own money most of the time and she got some other sponsors besides us to help her out. I hope she keeps doing well in the new class so she doesn't lose them."

"Well, last year was her first really big year," Mary replied. "Running street stock doesn't attract a lot of sponsors. Getting into the pro stock class should help her with that."

Jim had worked for ten years in a local Chevy dealership and was considered the best mechanic there. Then he decided to go off on his own. He and his wife struggled for quite a few years to put together enough money to start their business. With his well-deserved reputation, many customers followed him to his new business and it was now beginning to pay off. As Sam had gotten older Jim brought her along into the business and taught her a lot about repairing cars.

Sam was a fast learner. She didn't care for school that much, but all her teachers knew that their automobiles would be fixed properly if they put them in the care of Sam and her father. In school she spent most of her time drawing elaborate pictures of racecars. She loved her art classes and perfected her drawing skills under the instruction of her favorite teacher, Mr. Brock. He would shake his head in wonder as Sam would turn out one masterpiece after another.

For an art class project Sam created a whole book of pictures of her favorite NASCAR cars, complete with the drivers standing next to their cars. One year Sam's collection won first prize at the annual school art show. At Mr. Brock's suggestion, she submitted it to the annual county fair art show and again won first prize. Mr. Brock said he thought it was good enough to take to a publisher if she just changed a few things. Sam told him she would work on the changes but just didn't have the time with work and racing and all. When prodded by Mr. Brock, Sam would reply, "Yep, I'm going to do it but not right now, I have to race this weekend."

Mr. Brock understood and just smiled at his star art student.

After Sam had graduated from high school, Mr. Brock made it a point to stop by to see Sam at the shop and worked into the conversation the subject of the proposed book. She would always listen politely but somehow never managed to get back to work on it.

April in the northeast could be cold and rainy with a few beautiful warm days thrown in here and there. This April was no exception.

Sam displayed her car in all the pre-season street car shows at local shopping malls. Her skill at bodywork combined with her artwork on her number three car was always a real crowd pleaser. Sam's cars always looked nice. Coats of wax were applied to the finished surface and they were buffed to make the cars shine even more. Sam was proud of her work and it was good for business. Many of her fans became good customers.

The shows were fun but Sam was ready to race.

CHAPTER THREE

Sam was happy to see that her new pro stock car was ready. At least it was as ready as she could make it without trying it out on a track. Nobody could set up a car perfectly without trying it out first. She knew that computers were being used to design suspension setups and engine characteristics on expensive NASCAR Cup cars and other racecars, but the average car owner racing on Saturday night just didn't have the money or the facilities for that. Still, it was a far cry from the street stock wreck she had ended the season with the year before.

It was Saturday and Sam looked up at the clock and saw it was almost noon — quitting time. She had been edgy all morning and now it was almost time to get ready to leave for the track. She wanted to get to the track by 3:00 p.m.

She looked over the hood of the car she was working on and suddenly her heart jumped — it had begun to rain. *Oh no*, she thought. The first chance to test out her car and now the track might close because of rain. Just about all racetracks had practice days before the season started and drivers counted on these practice days to work on their cars, tuning the engine and checking the handling to make sure they were ready for competition. Sam was no exception. She had just built her car and now she needed the time to fine-tune it to make sure everything worked and the handling was where she wanted it to be. She needed to check the brakes, the shifters, the engine, the handling — everything. It was hard to check all those details until the car could be run on a track.

Testing was crucial to a race car. NASCAR drivers and their teams spent weeks testing at various tracks before the first race of the season at Daytona Speedway. Many teams had enough money to rent track time for testing. Sam had no money for that and her competitors didn't have it either.

The Fonda track had a warm-up race each spring and many of the teams came in to test and set up their cars. This race did not have any points awarded and was reserved for testing. Of course the drivers still pushed to see if they could beat their last year's competitors.

That warm-up race day was very important to all, but most important to those like Sam who had new cars. Old cars were usually okay with the set-up from the year before, needing only minor adjustments. Sam and Dave had set up the new pro stock car pretty similar to the old street stock car, but a lot of minor adjustments would have to be made. That warm-up race was crucial.

Sam watched the weather forecast very carefully the week before the test day, but couldn't be sure of the forecast because it called for mixed clouds and possibly rain. The weather in the spring in New York was very unpredictable. Farmers prayed for rain, but were afraid of too much rain as they wouldn't be able to get their machines on the fields to prepare for planting.

In upstate New York farm country the main topic of conversation in the spring was always "the weather." It was a great topic because the weather was always changing. It could mean an occasional dry spell giving crops a slow start or torrential rains that flooded and softened the fields and made it impossible to plant. Quite severe snow storms could also come up, stopping traffic and closing schools for a couple of days. The snow usually wouldn't last because it was often followed by bright sunny days that melted it all away quickly.

And now, rain. Sam could only hope the rain would stop in time to prepare the track for the evening practice race. They needed about six hours to prepare and dry the dirt track before allowing cars on.

Sam proceeded as if the practice session was on and that the rain would stop before the track got too soggy. She hooked up the trailer to her pickup truck. The truck was an '85 Ford F250 with a Cleveland 351 engine and 4 speed manual transmission that she bought for five hundred dollars from a local farmer. It had been in bad shape and she completely restored it. A complete body job removed all the dents and rust. She painted it and put in a new interior and pulled and rebuilt the engine. She also reworked the engine a little so it was putting out even more horsepower than when it was new. With the addition of headers and aftermarket mufflers, it sounded real nice and had plenty of power to pull her street stock car on the trailer. It looked like it had just come off the showroom floor and was an attraction by itself when she pulled into the races.

It was only drizzling so she continued to prepare for the race. She started the racecar and drove it onto the trailer. She listened to the roar of the finely tuned and high-spirited engine that Jack had built for her and smiled. The engine sounded really good and strong. She knew she wouldn't have to worry too much about the engine, only the handling of the car. The engine had been completely torn down and rebuilt by her friend Jack and she knew it would hold its own against any other car on the track. She just had to make sure the car would stay on the track by fine-tuning the suspension and handling. She stabbed the throttle a few times to hear the roar and then shut it down. It sounded great and she was happy. Sam then packed the trailer and truck box with all the tools she thought she would need for the practice session. She packed some extra spare parts, as she wasn't too sure about the adjustments she would have to make. Only running time on the track would determine that.

Dave came into Sam's area wiping his hands on a shop rag. "Hey, Sam," he called out. "Your mom called and said she drove by the track and said they had the "Track Closed" sign out."

"Oh, damn," Sam called back. "I needed that practice time. I have no idea how it's going to handle. Now I'll have to wait until next Saturday's warm ups before the race.

"You're right — not really enough time," Dave said as he shrugged his shoulders, "but you have to do what you have to do. Remember a lot of the other drivers at the first race will be in the same boat."

"Yeah, but some of them ran their cars last year and know what the setup should be," Sam said.

"Take the good with the bad, Sam," Dave said. "We'll work it out."

"Yeah, I know," she said as she turned to unload everything she had just put on the trailer.

Dave helped Sam unload the trailer and put all the tools back on the shelves where they belonged. She was not in a good mood; she had waited all winter for this opportunity. Barring sickness or injury, nothing in a young racer's life was worse than a rainout.

Unfortunately, it rained all weekend.

Much to her father's delight, Sam decided to clean the garage to wile away the time. All week long stuff accumulated in a garage. There was always cleaning to do, and for Sam, cleaning made the weekend go faster.

She thought about Chuck, who had abandoned all hope of running this year. She missed him. He came home some weekends, which brought him to her for dates and Sunday dinners at her mom and dad's, but he was often preoccupied with business and didn't have a lot of time for her. For the first time in her life she understood the old expression, "Absence makes the heart grow fonder." They had been together so much since high school that she hardly remembered life without him.

They were a great couple. They liked many of the same things, enjoyed the same books. Often they would recommend books for each other and purchase them for gifts for one another. It was the same with movies. Usually their dates would involve taking in a movie at the local theater and laughing or crying about the same passages afterward. They got a kick out of that and often were amused by that fact. They truly enjoyed being together and very seldom argued. It made their relationship an easy one.

CHAPTER FOUR

In a race driver's mind nothing beats the excitement of the first race of the season. The nights before the race were usually restless and sometimes sleepless as drivers and crew members tossed and turned worrying about the fitness of the car.

They all wondered if they had thought of everything: if every last bolt, screw, and nut had been tightened and checked; if the gas cans were filled; if the spare tires were pressurized properly and re-checked; If there was spare oil in case an oil line popped; if the radiator was okay and not leaking — had it been pressurized to check that no water oozed out anywhere. Those were some of the questions that disturbed sleep and drove racing teams nuts.

Sam was no different, though she was confident that what Dave hadn't thought of, she had. Sam was a pacer. She'd wake up and pace the floor in her apartment until she just gave up and went back to bed for a couple of hours of restless sleep.

She was up early on Saturday and was well on her way to loading the spare parts and equipment into the truck and trailer by the time the shop opened. She left the car off the trailer in case Dave or she wanted to do some last minute repairs or changes.

Her father came down to the shop at eight o'clock and looked over the scene. "No problem getting out of bed this morning, eh, Sam? Looks like you're ready to go."

"Yeah, Dad, I didn't sleep too well last night and got up around five, so I'd have plenty of time to load and go through everything in my mind."

"Well, good luck today. Mom and I will come down later in the afternoon."

"Thanks, Dad, I appreciate that and thanks for all the help this winter — all that time I needed to take off to run for parts and stuff."

"No problem, Sam. Your racing with the shop name on the sides helps the business and keeps us busy."

Sam and her father discussed the appointments for the day as Dave drove up. "Hey, did you sleep last night?" he said.

Sam smiled. "No; did you?"

"Not much," Dave replied and they both laughed.

Jim was amused by the conversation. "You better take an alarm clock with you so the two of you don't sleep through the races."

Sam smiled, "Hey! Good idea, Dad."

The three moved to start the day's work.

That afternoon, Sam was ready to go. At least she was as ready as she could be without track time with the new car. The weather was sunny and mild with not a cloud in the sky. She had stripped down to a tee shirt for the first time this spring and she still perspired a little as she worked.

She had checked and double-checked everything that might go wrong. Her and Dave's years of experience indicated that they had eliminated almost all possible mechanical problems. Handling was the only question in their minds and they could do very little about that until practice laps at the track.

Sam subscribed to the old tried and true theory that "loose is fast" and she set up most of her racecars that way. She knew other racers, including Chuck Turner, believed that also and the theory was proven time after time at dirt tracks around the country. A car that easily went sideways in the turns in a controlled skid was usually always the faster car. The key word was "control" — the driver had to be able to control the skid — something Chuck needed to concentrate on, she thought.

Sam believed that Chuck Turner ran his car too loose, which had put Sam out of the last race and cost her a racecar last year. It was a car she hated to lose because she ran in the top five in just about every race and won a lot of them as well. But then, she probably wouldn't have moved to pro stock if she still had her old street stock car, so she was satisfied. Besides, building the new pro stock car had made the cold and snowy winter months fly by.

∽

Soon it was time to head for the track. She and Dave went over all her lists of spares and "must do" items. They felt that they had not missed anything. Dave helped her toggle the car to the trailer and they were on their way.

As they approached the pit gate they greeted and shouted out to all the familiar faces there waiting for the gate to open.

"Hey, Sam, welcome to pro stock," Bill Wilson called out to her. "My old car looks better than it ever did."

"It took lots of elbow grease," she replied, as she greeted her old pal.

Now that he wasn't racing, Bill had taken a job at the pit gate. He missed the racing and now could see all his friends and competitors as they entered.

"You going to miss the scene?" she asked.

"Oh, sure, but I'm keeping busy, as you can see. I'm so happy I could help you get into pro stock, sweetheart. I know you'll do well and I'll be watching you. If there is anything I can do for you, just let me know."

"Thanks a lot, old pal; I sure will let you know if I need some advice and help."

Bill nodded. "It'll take a little time to get going, but I think you'll do okay. You have to get used to the increased power and learn not to baby it. Just keep a steady pace and you'll love it; I can tell. The pro stock drivers sure are talking about you. I think they're worried that you'll do to them what you did to everyone in street stock."

Sam and Bill both laughed and Dave, sitting next to her in the passenger seat, laughed along with them.

"I hope so but I've got to get some seat time in before I set this world on fire."

"You'll do just fine, Hon. Okay; here are your passes. Have fun."

Sam found a pit area spot near some friends and she and Dave unloaded. They organized everything to their liking, warmed up the car, and waited.

Sam heard the track steward calling out the numbers for the first practice laps and her number came up. It was time to strap on her helmet. She climbed in through the driver side window and settled into the seat that she and

Dave had carefully placed just right for Sam's size and driving style. Dave helped her settle in and fasten her safety harness. She leaned forward into the harness and adjusted the tightness of the straps to her liking. She flipped up the ignition switch and then the starter switch and the car roared to life immediately. She smiled as she felt the powerful vibrations running through the car. She knew the engine would not fail her. Jack knew what he was doing.

Sam smiled and thought about how much she loved this — the friends, the cars, and noise around her as others gunned their engines to move into position at the track entrance. She loved the smell of the track and the dirt. Fonda Speedway was one of the oldest tracks in the country and it had been there for over fifty years. The dirt — mostly clay — had been saturated with oil, gas, exhaust fumes, and tiny chunks of tire rubber over those years. All that mixed together gave the air around the track the smell that dirt track racers loved.

Her heart raced and her palms inside her driving gloves felt a little sweaty as she contemplated the coming contest. Even though she was nervous she felt totally at home here. All her years of racing on this track gave her a confidence that she loved.

The track entrance worker signaled the next group in. Sam pressed in the clutch and slid the shift lever into second. She let out the clutch and the car jumped into motion, rear wheels spinning slightly. She backed off the gas to avoid rear-ending the car in front of her. The power of the new car was awesome and still surprised her a little.

She had decided to make two laps at moderate speed to check the handling in the corners and then push it for the remaining four or five laps.

The crowd of cars thinned as the more aggressive drivers pushed their 450 horsepower motors to the limit almost immediately. Sam got caught up in the excitement. She realized she had to push harder than she really wanted to in order to avoid getting rear-ended by the more aggressive drivers behind her.

The first turn came up on her fast.

Oh, boy, I hope I can get this baby sideways or I'll be into the wall on the first lap.

The rear end slid out and Sam fought to keep it under control. She feared it was too loose as the back end wanted to catch up with the front. Other cars flew by her as she struggled in the upper, muddier part of the track. She came out of turn two and pressed the pedal to the metal. She was amazed how the car bit in and leaped ahead on the straightaway. She passed two of the cars that had passed her in the corner. She wasn't used to all the power of the newly-freshened pro stock engine and she was impressed. Dave had done a great job of tuning the new engine. She realized that if she could get her cornering under control she would have a fantastic racecar.

Turn three was coming up fast and she knew she would have to stay low and "in the groove" to make sure the car stayed controllable. The "groove" was the most packed and driest part of the track; usually low in the turn going in and then spreading out wider as more and more cars packed it down as the night progressed.

The two cars she had passed on the straight were now bearing down on her and she knew she had to push it into the turn even though she didn't feel good about that. Again, she fought the car to keep the rear wheels from coming around too far. She just barely kept her position and then opened up more distance on the on the front straight.

She finished the fourth lap and decided to get off the track before she crashed in one of the corners. She had an idea of what she had to do to make the car handle better so she pulled back into the pit area.

Dave came running over as Sam killed the engine. "Oh boy, I know what we have to do. You've got fantastic power in the straights, but it's a horrible monster in the corners. Your arms were flying around so fast in the turns you looked like you were making milkshakes and swatting flies in there all at the same time," he laughed. "Chuck would have loved to see you flailing around like he did in his car most of the time."

Sam laughed with him as she pulled off her helmet. "Wow, what a ride," she said as she ran her hand through her damp hair. "What a workout! Look at me. Four laps and I'm starting to sweat already. At least we know there's nothing wrong with the power steering and the engine. In that first turn I thought I was going to get to know the guy running the ice-cream stand on the other side of the wall really well."

They both laughed and Sam climbed out of the car.

She clapped Dave on the back. "Let me tell you, you and Jack did a great job on that engine. That thing runs like a bear."

"Yeah, I wish I could have seen the eyes of those two guys who passed you in turns one and two when you passed them on the straight. They looked like they had their feet on the brakes instead of on the gas."

"Yep, we got the power side pretty much taken care of. Now, what should we do about the cornering? I think maybe we ought to add some more weight on the inside back wheel. I just need more bite on that left side. I'm way too loose. I thought I was done for sure in the first turn on that first lap."

"Sounds good to me," Dave replied. "Now's the time to experiment. If that engine is as good as you say, it probably needs some help to keep her down in the corners."

Dave went to the spare parts box and pulled out two ten-pound weights while Sam jacked up the car. Dave then bolted the weights on to the small stack already on the left rear.

He looked at Sam as he finished. "You think twenty pounds is enough — too much, maybe? What do you think?"

Sam thought a minute. "Let's try the twenty for qualifying and see how we do. We can adjust from there. We'll use tonight for testing. Next week we'll go for points.

"I agree; we'll go after those guys for sure next week."

They then checked and double-checked everything they could think of. Dave removed all the spark plugs and checked their color. If they were too dark or too light, the jets in the carburetor would have to be changed. If they were light tan, they would be good — and they were.

The numbers were called for qualifying and it was time to suit up and get going again. Sam's heat would qualify five cars and Sam had to be in that top five or she would have to run the consolation race. They felt ready. Sam was anxious to try the new set-up in the turns and gunned onto the track for the warm-up lap.

The cars took a lap, then the green flag came out and Sam was ready for it. She slammed the throttle down. She was already in third gear. She was off and to her surprise the car held in the first turn and she didn't lose an inch. She realized that she and Dave had made the right choice by placing twenty more pounds on the left rear.

She powered out of the second turn and passed two cars in the back straight. She knew she would be passing a couple more cars on the front straight. But as she punched it out of the second turn she heard and felt a sickening thump coming from the rear of her car. She almost lost it as the car twisted from right to left and back again as she spun the wheel fighting for control.

From past experience, she knew exactly what had happened. She had broken an axle. In an attempt to cut costs, she and Dave used the street stock axles instead of buying expensive, high tech ones. They just neglected to take into consideration the increased power going to them from the higher performance engine. That would be it for them that night, as they had no spares.

Sam felt embarrassed as she accepted a tow back into the pits. She had failed to look ahead to all the problems that might come. She and Dave had missed this one. Dave would share the blame, but Sam knew it was mainly her responsibility. Disappointed, they loaded the car and the tools back onto the trailer. The rest of the night would be spent sitting with their friends in the bleachers watching others race while they stewed over their mistake.

Dave clapped her on the back. "Next week, we'll be ready for everything. The way you looked out there I know we'll do well."

Sam smiled, "Yep, always next week. We just have to keep saying that or we'll go nuts. Let's go find the gang and we'll watch with them for a while."

They found their friends in the stands and sat with them. She missed Chuck and looked for her old school chum, Allison.

Allison smiled. "Sam, I saved a couple of seats for you guys over here. What happened? You were doing so well. We all thought you'd win easy."

She and Dave moved into the seats Allison had saved. Sam moved over to Allison's side and turned her hands palm up and shrugged her shoulders.

"Can't win 'em all," she said. Sam explained the broken axle.

"What a shame. You were doing so well," Allison exclaimed. "You definitely would have finished in the top five and qualified for the final. You sure looked good out there. I'll bet you could've won."

Sam nodded her head in agreement. "I'm sure I could have gotten into the top five, too. Winning, though? I'm not so sure. I'm really not used to the car yet."

Allison patted Sam on the arm. "I know you would have won. You were going by cars like crazy."

"Well, maybe. We'll find out for sure next week."

Allison had been a friend since high school. They would often work together in study halls and their friendship had remained through graduation and beyond. Sam had little time for her friend, but they often skied together at Royal Mountain on Sundays.

Allison graduated from the local community college after high school and became an administrative assistant at a law firm in a city about forty miles away. Their friendly relationship remained, but the forty miles was difficult for Sam to overcome. Allison made sure that she got to most of Sam's races so she could touch bases with her friend. Not only were they very close and enjoyed each other's company, they could always confide in one another and any time either one had any problems they were only a phone call away.

CHAPTER FIVE

They went on to finish tenth the next week and then as Sam got used to the car, she finished regularly in the top five or ten and even won a couple of races. This was greeted with joy by her, Dave, and their supporters who gathered in her pit area after every race. Even though they didn't finish as winners every week, they kept finishing high enough to lead the chase for points in the pro stock class.

Whenever Dave asked if he could help with anything she always told him just to keep on doing whatever he was already doing. "The car is perfect just like it is," she said as she gave him a big hug. "You don't need to do a thing except keep the gas tank full."

And that's what he did. Once in a while he installed a new set of tires or new spark plugs but that was about it. He was a believer in preventive maintenance and thoroughly checked out everything between races. His painstaking efforts made Sam a very happy stockcar driver.

Once in a while Sam would come across a so-called tough customer who would try to bully her or push her off the track in a corner, but her superior driving skill and the power and smooth handling of the car enabled her to steer clear of trouble. Usually these drivers came from rival tracks and had heard stories about Sam's fame and they sought her out to test their skills against hers. They went back to their home tracks with stories about the famous female driver and those stories only enhanced Sam's image.

Chuck went to as many races as he could. "Hey, Sam, you're on your way to the big time. You look great out there. I'm really impressed."

They never had serious problems, but little ones plagued them now and then. One week it was a flat tire in the main. They always raced on a shoe string and the tire that blew was one they thought they could get one more race out of. In a long race, it was possible to change a tire and get back in and finish a race but in a weekly ten-lapper, by the time you changed a tire the race was pretty much over.

In the beginning of the season the oil pressure gauge kept registering low and Sam pulled out of a couple of races not wanting to take the chance that she would blow the engine. They finally figured out that the oil was flowing to the right side of the engine on the sharp corners of the short track and the oil pump couldn't pick up the oil it needed for complete lubrication of the engine. They solved that problem by installing a connecting hose between the left and right sides of the engine to equalize the oil level on both sides.

If the minor problems occurred in a heat race, they could be fixed in time to run in the LCQ (Last Chance Qualifier).

During the main of another race, Sam ran out of gas. In the pits they couldn't figure what was wrong and looked in vain for a leak in the gas line somewhere. Finally, Sam looked at Dave and asked him, "Did you …?"

Dave looked at Sam and said, "No, did you …?"

They looked at each other and started laughing. They had gotten a late start from the shop that day and in the rush to get to the track neither one of them had thought to check the gas level in the car.

One week a collision with another car almost in last place messed up the steering in the main. Another week the transmission failed and had to be replaced.

After the races, the number three pit area was filled with autograph seekers and potential sponsors stopped by and asked if they could help out with some money. Soon almost every available space was filled on Sam's car. Many customers came to the Taylors' shop because of the fame of the number three and Sam.

Everything was going very nicely for the number three car. Everyone involved in the effort was very happy, including Sam's mom and dad who attended every race and cheered their daughter on.

 ∽

Chuck Turner was busy with his dad in the trucking business and didn't have time to race, but he did had have time to come to the races when he was in town and watch his girlfriend. He saw Sam's impressive skill as she powered by just about everyone on the track unless, of course, she had a problem. Her skill was obvious as she worked herself around or through mixups and smashups.

Business was going well for Chuck. The new additional truck line in the south was paying off. Every week she raced he paid her for an ad that displayed the Turner Trucking signs on the car. "At least I can give you enough to buy you a couple of tires now and then."

Hey, no problem," Sam said as the two shared a laugh. "I've got a couple of dead beats on here and I'll just paint over them and make the Turner Trucking sign bigger."

"By the way, what kind of rinky-dink operation are you guys running here? You'd win every race if it wasn't for flat tires, oil leaks, and radiator problems. I could do better with one hand tied behind my back," Chuck teased.

"Low budget operation. That's what we have here. We can't afford top shelf like some people I know," Sam said with a grin. "By the way, are you going to race this year or not? Give me advance warning if you are. I'll put some extra armor on my car, and stay away from you in the corners."

"Very funny," Chuck said with a grin. "I'm just too busy. That outfit we bought down south will take our territory clear down to South Carolina. My plate is too full. No time to race. We're operating from Maine almost to the Georgia border now. It's nice to see the business grow, but it sure does take a lot of time and effort. I'm still travelling a lot down south to take care of new customers. We're making money, but it's no good for my racing. I don't even have time to work on the car and the guys in the shop are working long hours so they don't have time to help me, either. I think my racing days might be over."

Sam placed her hand on his shoulder. "Come on, Chuck, you've got to have some good times with all that hard work."

"Yeah, I wish. I'll just have to wait and get my fun out of watching you whenever I can. It's not as much fun as being out there with you. You know, this is the first time I haven't been out there with you in about six years."

"I know, I miss having you banging into me on every corner," Sam said with a laugh; "maybe next year."

"Yeah, maybe next year, but I think play time is over for this boy. Dad definitely wants to retire and that means more work on my desk. So I'll just have to get all my racing kicks out of watching you on Saturday nights whenever I can. Also, if everything in the business keeps going the way it is, how about letting us be your only sponsor next year – along with your dad, of course?"

"That's fine with me. It sure could save me a lot of time running around and lining up sponsors before next season." Sam gazed up into her boyfriend's eyes. "I think it's great that you want to do that, Chuck. I really appreciate it. Also, it would be nice to work with someone who really knows how much it costs to enter a car and keep it running."

CHAPTER SIX

Sam sat straight up in bed. She had awakened from a sound sleep. The fire alarm system that she and her dad installed in the shop downstairs had gone off.

As soon as she realized that the often-tested alarm would not go off unless there was a fire, she leaped out of bed. Her heart was pounding and she was frightened. She could hear the pop and sizzle of the fire below and felt heat coming through the window. It was obviously a bad fire.

"Sam, Sam! Get out of there," she heard her father yelling. Sam slipped on her work boots and a jacket and cautiously checked to see if the exit door was hot to the touch before she opened it. The fire seemed to be mainly on the other side of the shop and Sam's deck and the stairway down to the ground appeared safe.

Her father was already up on the deck racing for the door as she opened it. Sam burst out and almost ran into him.

"Come on, sweetheart, let's get out of here. It looks like the whole thing's going to go. When all that paint we've got stored starts to go, she's a goner."

"Dad, did you call 911?"

"Yes, Mom did when I went out the door. Let's get the garden hoses out and water down this side of the house. At least maybe we can save that."

They ran toward the house and Sam grabbed her father's arm and stopped him. "Dad, can I get my car out?"

Jim stopped and put his hand on his daughter's shoulder. "No," he said with sorrow in his voice, "the fire is the worst where your car is."

"Oh, no," Sam cried. "I'm going to have to start all over."

"Sam, you're safe and that's all I care about. We'll build you another race car."

Sam shook her head. She thought about her winning season going up in smoke. She turned for an instant to see the flames behind the windows where her car was parked and knew her father was right. She was heartsick and near tears over the whole situation. She knew her father was insured for the fire but her car wasn't.

"OK, Dad, I'm with you; let's at least save the house."

She looked up and saw her mother on the porch. She ran up the stairs and gave her a quick hug and told her, "Don't worry, Mom, we'll be okay."

She ran back down the stairs to help her father. They soon had two hoses hooked up and were soaking the side of the house that faced the now-blazing shop. They weren't sure low long they could stand the intense heat from the fire. They could hear the sirens as the fire trucks approached.

Mini explosions could now be heard as overheated paint cans exploded and added more fuel to the fire now leaping upstairs through Sam's apartment. Sam could feel the intense heat on her face and turned away to concentrate on wetting down the house.

Her mind was racing and tears were running down her cheeks as she thought of all the personal items that she would lose. *Dad and I worked so hard to build that apartment*, she thought.

Fortunately, her mother had insisted on keeping most of her art work at the house because she loved to look at it. Mr. Brock will be happy, she thought.

Suddenly, the yard was filled with flashing red and blue lights as fire trucks and police cars rolled into the yard. Firemen with coats shimmering with fluorescent striping were running here and there. Big flood lights were set up so the men could see what they were doing.

One group pulled out hoses from the truck and advanced toward Sam and Jim to help them wet down the side of the house. Yet another group was hooking up the pumper truck to a hydrant nearby. They were volunteers, but each knew what they were doing and they did it quickly and efficiently.

Sam and Jim knew each one of them by their first names. That's the way it is in a small town.

"Rotten luck, Sam, Jim," one yelled.

Sam and her dad just nodded their heads. They turned off their hoses as water from the pumper truck cascaded down the side of the house. They knew the house would be saved.

Jim and Sam approached Chief Stoddard as he raised his megaphone to his lips. "No heroics, guys. She's a goner. Just keep her cool and contained," his voice boomed out.

"Gotcha, Chief," someone yelled. Others waved that they had heard him.

He turned to look at the sad faces of Sam and Jim. "Sorry about this, Jim. It's a shame. I know how hard you guys worked to build this business."

"Nobody got hurt, that's the main thing." said Jim. "I'm so glad we put in that alarm system for Sam that you told us about."

"Woke me up, for sure," Sam added. "Thanks for the advice, Chief."

Chief Stoddard looked at her. "Your car was in there, wasn't it?"

"Yeah," Sam replied, "we finally had it set up perfect."

Chief Stoddard was a race fan and hardly missed any of Sam's races. He sadly shook his head. "Too bad; you've been running really well. You guys going to rebuild?"

"Sure am," Jim replied. "I've worked too hard at this to just walk away. I think I have enough insurance to build another shop."

"Good," the chief said. "I like having a dependable shop that's going to take good care of our trucks and cars," he said smiling.

"Thanks, Chief."

Chief Stoddard turned back to the fire. "Jim, if I remember, most of the paint was stored in that right hand bay, right?" he asked.

"Yeah, Chief, right in front of Sam's car." he put his arm around his daughter.

The Chief raised the megaphone again and explained the situation to his men. "Break out the windows in that bay on the right and pour it on. Be careful, there's a lot of paint stored in there and we want to cool it down if we can."

The lead man on the hose raised his hand that he understood and advanced toward the bay. Another fireman took a long pike pole and broke out the windows and the hose crew poured water into the bay.

Suddenly, several loud cracks were heard from inside as the building started to cave in. What used to be Sam's apartment came crashing down into the fiery ruins of the shop as sparks and flaming wood flew through the air threatening the firemen.

"Back away; back away!" Chief Stoddard shouted to his men through his megaphone. "She's going down!"

They all backed away and watched helplessly as the building groaned and collapsed slowly on top of itself.

That did it for Sam and Jim. Tears of deep sorrow rolled down their faces as they felt small but strong arms around their necks. Sam turned to see her mother standing between them. She was crying, too. Sam and her father moved so they could put their arms around Mary.

Neighbors appeared with steaming cups of coffee. Arms reached out to join the family and the little group grew as neighbors and friends appeared to offer comfort to the Taylors.

The minutes turned to hours. The fire department worked to contain the blaze and pour water on the paint storage area to keep it cool and put out what flames they could. Other firemen stood by with hoses ready to stop little flare-ups here and there.

As the sun came up the firemen began the job of cleaning up and rolling up the hoses. A more thorough job of cleaning would be done when they got back to the firehouse.

Chief Stoddard came over to Jim and Sam. "Well, that about wraps it up. If you get a flare-up give us a call, but I think we got it all. I'll leave a small crew here for awhile just in case. Not much left to burn anyway with all that paint taking off like it did. Not too much you can do about that except keep it cooled down."

"Thanks, Chief; I'm so glad you guys saved the house. We can rebuild the shop."

"Jim, even if we had been right around the corner, I don't think we could have saved the shop. Automobile paint out of the can is some of the toughest stuff to put out. I'll get the county fire inspector out here as quick as I can. I know you'll want to rebuild as soon as possible."

Jim replied, "I appreciate that, Chief."

"No problem, Jim. I'll stop by tomorrow after you have had a chance to pull yourselves together."

Jim turned and looked at Sam and a smile came over his face.

"What's so funny, Dad?" she asked.

Jim started to laugh hard. "No pants," he blurted out.

"What?" Sam replied.

"No pants, you're still in the shorts you slept in!"

"Uh, oh," Sam said as she looked down at the pair with little balloons all over them, and then at her neighbors who were laughing, too. "I didn't have time for pants." And she joined in the laughter.

Jim put his arm around Sam and pulled her closer. "That's okay, Hon, we're together and nobody got hurt. That's the main thing."

Mary tugged on Sam's arm and led her into the house. "Come inside, you have some pants in the wash and I'll whip up some breakfast for us."

CHAPTER SEVEN

Later that morning, Sam walked out to the leveled and still-smoking shop. She stood looking in the stall that contained her Number Three. She could still make out the blackened, charred number "3" on the crushed car. Strange, she thought. She vowed that number "3" would stay with her for the rest of her life. She had barely driven it, but she knew it was the best car she had ever owned and she vowed she would never forget it. That car had been the final proof of her skill as a racecar driver. It had performed well.

Tears came again as she looked at the scorched remains. Everything in the car was ruined — her custom seat, steering wheel, fuel cell — all gone. She assumed the engine was ruined, too, from the awful heat that had engulfed the car.

She had left her driving suit, helmet, and gloves in the car and they, of course, were gone as well. The scene was dulled and her vision blurred as tears flooded from her eyes. *I'm done for this year*, she thought. *How could I ever afford to build another one like this?* She and her folks had very little savings and she could never put together enough money for another car.

She felt a gentle arm around her shoulders and turned to see Dave standing beside her with tears running down his face as well. "I came as soon as I heard the news," he said. "How awful. It's so hard to believe."

She turned into Dave's arms and cried into his chest. "I can't believe it either," she sobbed.

The breakfast table was very quiet that morning. All three were lost in their own thoughts. There was no daily schedule to discuss or problems to address, and though there were plenty of calls to make, none of them had the strength to talk. Once in a while, the tears would start again but they comforted each other until the tears stopped. They faced a difficult day.

Sam knew she should call Chuck, who was in North Carolina for the week. She wanted him to hear the bad news from her and not someone else.

"Okay, Dad, any ideas what caused it?".

Jim pondered the question as he leaned back in his chair. "Well," he said, "with any fire, the first thoughts are electrical shorts, furnace, spontaneous combustion, vandalism, or fraud. We know fraud is out of the question; we certainly wouldn't set fire to a business that means so much to us," he said. "Darned if I know for sure. Maybe a short in the wiring, maybe spontaneous combustion from some oily rags we had laying around and forgot about or maybe vandalism. As much as we don't like to think about it, maybe somebody set it on fire on purpose. But no matter what we think, the final judges are the investigators and the insurance company adjusters. Hopefully, the adjusters will figure it out. We need to know so we don't make the same mistake again."

"Dad, come on, everybody knows we wouldn't do anything like that on purpose."

"Yes, we know that, but the ones investigating the fire don't."

"And, Dad, they have to know that you would never start a fire under your own daughter's apartment." She smiled. "At least I don't think you would."

Her father gave her a look. "That's not funny, Sam; don't even joke about it."

"I'm sorry, Dad; just trying to lighten things up. So, we know we didn't do it on purpose; what's next?"

"Electrical, furnace, spontaneous combustion, or vandalism is about all that's left. I just had the furnace cleaned last fall before the heating season and I think the wiring is in good shape. I'm pretty careful about leaving piles of oily rags lying around. How about you?

"Dad, you've lectured me a thousand times about that." She paused and thought. Her face drooped. "Oh, oh, I just remembered I did throw some oily rags in a box in front of my car. Maybe I left them there. I hope that wasn't it."

Jim looked at his daughter. "Well, too late now for regrets. They'll be going over the ash heap out there with a fine tooth comb. If that was it they'll find it, Sweetheart. Don't worry."

Sam felt terrible anyway. She was afraid that her carelessness might have burned down the business that the whole family had worked so hard to build.

Her father noticed Sam's distress and changed the subject. "Let's make a list of everything that has to be done. Why don't you guys start on the list and I'll call the insurance company to report the fire. It's nine a.m. so they should be open by now.

Sam pulled out her cell phone. "I've got to call Chuck; then Mom and I can start on the list." This was not a call she wanted to make.

After the call, Sam and her mother got started and by the time Jim returned the list was long and they agreed that they had not thought of everything.

"The lifts have to be replaced and we have to have one bay big enough to hold large trucks and RVs. Also, all our tools will have to be replaced including the spin balancer, the tire changer, spray booth, spray guns, and air compressors. I can't believe it," Jim said and heaved a big sigh. "All that stuff is gone."

"It's a long list, Dad; we probably should start calling suppliers soon to get some prices for insurance."

"Yep, and how about the building? We have to design that and think about what kind to put up. Should we do a steel building or bring in carpenters to do a custom stick built?"

"Steel will be faster, Dad, maybe we should look at that first."

"Yeah, you're right, but maybe we can call some local carpenters for their ideas. You and I can work right along with them."

As they finished breakfast, the three looked at each other and felt sad again.

"All that hard work went up in smoke. Everything is gone in just a few hours," Jim said shaking his head.

Mary could see the two of them needed a pep talk.

"Hey, you two just look at it this way. We still have a great bunch of customers. They'll come back as soon as we start up again. Also, you always wanted to replace the lifts and wanted at least one bay that was high enough to service RVs and trucks. Maybe the insurance will cover that.

You always wanted a new, more modern air compressor for the paint shop; maybe we can get one of those, too. We paid extra for full replacement value insurance so maybe everything will turn out okay."

Jim thought for a moment. "You're right, Mary, maybe it will all work out. The only thing that wasn't covered was Sam's car and we can always build her another when we get the shop rebuilt. Right, Sam?"

"Yeah, I guess so." Sam replied, "I hate to lose a whole season, but I guess we just have to be thankful that we're okay. And, Dad, maybe we can put up one of those steel buildings a lot faster than a stick built. Heck, we could be open for business again in a few weeks."

Mary was happy to see the two of them making plans and talking more positively. Their minds were thinking about the future instead of thinking about the fire.

They had a lot to do, but they were a hardworking family and this was not the first obstacle they had to overcome.

CHAPTER EIGHT

Jim answered the phone. It was Chief Stoddard saying that the fire investigators would be there first thing Monday morning.

"Thanks, Chief. I know you're working to get the investigation over with quickly so we can get back to work. I really appreciate your efforts."

Later that morning, Jim met with a contractor to arrange a date to clean up all the debris from the fire. Like in all small towns, the contractor was a friend, Frank Olsen.

Jim explained that they couldn't do anything until the adjusters give them the okay.

"Yeah, I know, Jim. I don't have too much going right now so I'll be ready when you are. What a mess, but we'll get her cleaned up. My new excavator is just the ticket for this job. It shouldn't take long at all. Everybody wants you back in business as soon as possible."

True to his word, the chief had gotten the arson investigators in that Monday and later that afternoon the adjusters came in and completed there investigation. After meeting with the adusters and the arson investigators, Chief Stoddard called Jim and told him to go ahead with the cleanup. Jim called Frank, his contractor friend, who was on the job the next morning with dump trucks, excavators, and a bobcat front end loader. Everything was going as planned.

Chief Stoddard told Sam and Jim that the cause had been "spontaneous combustion." They weren't sure exactly where it started, but for the rest of her life, Sam would wonder if it was her box of rags — her stupid mistake — that started the fire. Her father was kind to her and never mentioned it to her except for a brief pat on the back and a quiet, "We all make mistakes and we don't even know for sure if what you did was the cause. We'll probably never know."

Sam, Mary, and Jim met and talked to a couple of steel building manufacturers and to a few friends who were customers and made their living at carpentry. After long deliberation, they decided on a stick-built garage.

"If we do a stick built, we can work right along with them," Jim said. "That way we'll know it's done just the way we want it and we can save some money, too."

Sam agreed. "I can use something to keep me busy this winter so I don't spend all my time complaining and thinking about our losses. If we can start soon, we should be able to get a roof on before snow falls; then we can work on the inside all winter and hopefully be ready to open in the spring.

Sam, her father, and Frank Olsen met and planned out the building. They agreed that they needed five stalls — one for painting and four for general mechanical work — plus a half stall for an office with storage behind. They designed two of the bays at one end of the garage high enough to accommodate RVs and trucks. The first bay would be built high enough to make room for Sally's new apartment. She would have a clear view to the river running down in the valley below. They made the bays deep enough to accommodate two cars, a frame machine, and a wheel alignment ramp. "That'll be great for aligning the wheels on our stock cars," Sam chimed in. They planned so they would not have to do any additions in the future.

"This is it," Jim said with a laugh; "no more construction when this is done."

Sam and the contractor laughed. "Oh, yeah, don't forget my apartment," Sam joked.

The contractor's plan included walls and ceiling for Sam, but all the plumbing and electrical was not. Sam knew that she and her Dad could do that.

They had ordered a new sign. Sam had used her art talent to design it herself. It read "Taylor's Complete Auto Repair: Repairs from A to Z."

Everything was shaping up fast. The insurance settlement would cover almost everything and they were grateful that they had taken out as much insurance as they had. Jim had to borrow some additional money from the bank to get them back in the game, but not much.

CHAPTER NINE

Sam worked right along with her father and the other carpenters, but she was not 100 percent thrilled to be doing it. Carpentry wasn't her thing. She looked forward to racing in the spring. That's what carried her through the long New York winters. She worked to everyone's satisfaction and admiration, but basically she just put in her time doing what was asked and generally sharing the load with everyone else. She was a good worker, which covered up her sadness. She wanted to race in the spring and she couldn't get it out of her mind.

Sam kept Mr. Brock and everyone else happy by spending a lot of time working on her racecar book, which took her mind off the depression she felt. After making her mother promise not to say anything to her dad or anyone else, she confided how upset she was about not having a ride for the following season. Mom, as always, understood.

"I knew you weren't happy, Hon; you just don't have the enthusiasm you used to have."

"It's that obvious, Mom? I thought I was covering it up pretty good."

CHARLIE LOOMIS

"Just concentrate on the things you like," her mother said. "You love your art work and your book. Try to think about those things and don't worry about the racing. Who knows, maybe some miracle will happen and you'll be on the track again. Don't fret too much about things that are out of your control."

"Oh, Mom," Sam said, "what a dummy I am. I've been going on about my problems and forgot how the fire affected everybody else. You and Dad have worked so hard all your lives and all you accomplished went up in flames. I just never gave your worries a second thought."

"Yes, it is a big setback but I do exactly what I told you to do. I look at all the positives in my life. I have you and Daddy safe and sound, I have a nice house, and luckily I live with people who love me. Nobody was hurt in the fire and it looks like our insurance is going to take us almost back to normal. It'll take time, but if you keep looking at all the positives in your life that time will go fast. Also, don't forget about Chuck. Dad and I just love him and we think he is so good for you. You two are like peas in a pod. It's obvious he adores you and that's wonderful. Actually, when you consider everything, you're pretty lucky right now."

"You're right, Mom. And Mom, if I haven't told you lately, I really love you and Daddy and I am so lucky to have parents like you. I don't think too many parents would appreciate a daughter who loves to work on cars and race them. I'm really blessed. I'll just have to think more about those things. You know, I think I'll do some charcoals. I haven't done any in a long time. When I get tired of working on the book, I can go back to my sketches."

Mary smiled. "I can always find some wall space to hang more, Hon." She already had many of Sam's wonderful art works hanging in every room in the house and some pieces stored away that she hadn't even displayed yet. She loved all of them. When friends visited they always wanted to look at her collection and were impressed with Sam's artwork. Mary even sold some of Sam's paintings and kept the money for a secret college fund she had in case Sam ever wanted to go to college.

∽

The days wore on and the new garage took shape. Before the first snowfall, they got the roof and sidewalls done and then turned to work on the interior. They built the walls between some of the bays and even roughed in Sam's new apartment. Insulation and finishing the interior walls came next, along with installation of the heating units in each bay. Jim wanted individual units so he could close down bays that weren't used in the winter months when business slowed down.

Jim noticed that his daughter, though not really as light-hearted as she used to be, was becoming more cheerful and spirited. The work and the social time between them was good therapy. That and Mary's delivery of coffee and baked goods each morning kept all of them in good spirits.

If Chuck was in town, he often showed up around 10 o'clock for coffee and whatever Mary had baked. He kept everyone informed about how well the new southern branch of the family's trucking business was doing, which helped buoy Sam's spirits as well.

All the workers gently teased Sam when he left. "We can't expect too much work out of Sam for the rest of the day. She's love struck" … "Hey, Sam, did you and Chuck set the date yet? A wedding right here in the new building would be great" … they hollered out to her. Sam just smiled and nodded her head. She knew that any protest from her would just egg them on and make their teasing worse.

They were all Sam's supporters and admired her for her skills on the racetrack and her ability to hang with the best of them in whatever she was called upon to do. "Wow, she's amazing," they told Jim. "She's so tiny, but man, is she strong. She can swing a hammer and keep right up with us. No wonder she handles her racecars as well as she does." Jim would just nod his head beam with pride for his daughter.

Gradually the new building was completed, all the new equipment was delivered and installed, and at the end of each day, they could look with pride on their accomplishments. Sam was eagerly waiting for the time that her apartment was completed so that she and Chuck could have some time alone when he was in town. He still came to Sunday dinner whenever he could, but had very little time to spend with Sam as he had to leave as soon as he could to make the long drive to North Carolina.

CHAPTER TEN

It was time to make arrangements for the grand opening of the new shop. They decided on the first Saturday in April. They would drape the new building with crepe paper and brightly colored signs that Sam designed.

On the big day, the neighbors helped. They had already volunteered to pitch in when they heard about the big party. There were helium balloons for the kids and even second balloons to replace the ones that got away and soared up into the clear, blue sky. There was also hot dogs, chips, and soda for everyone.

It was a success and everyone enjoyed seeing the bright, new tool boxes in the repair bays and all the new equipment. It was a dream come true.

Dave looked at Sam. "Only one thing missing, buddy."

"What's that?" Sam replied.

"No shiny race car sitting in here."

"Yeah, wouldn't that be great. I could start it up and gas it for the kids. They'd love that."

"You got that right," Dave replied, "but we'll put something together, somehow. We'll think of something."

"Right, Dave, but whatever we think of better have money attached to it. Dad and I don't have two nickels to rub together until business starts coming into the shop."

"Okay, sometime next week we'll put our heads together and see what we come up with. Oh … oh, more kids around the balloons. I've got to go blow up some more. See ya later."

"Okay, Dave."

Sam looked up to see the friendly faces of Mr. and Mrs. Brock smiling at her. "You and your dad did a great job on the new place. Congratulations."

"Thanks, Mr. Brock. Great to see you guys. Did Mom and Allison hook you up with a hot dog?"

Mr. Brock gazed back at his favorite pupil. "They sure did, Sam. It was good, especially with your mom's famous meat sauce."

Mrs. Brock patted Sam on the arm. "The hot dog was delicious, Samantha and I must say, I agree with my husband. You and your dad did a wonderful job building the new shop. It looks so nice."

"Thanks, Mrs. Brock. I'm glad you like it. It was a lot of work but worth it."

Mr. Brock turned to Sam. "Say, I have to ask you, what are you going to do about a car this season?"

"Oh boy, that's a good question. We just haven't had time to talk about it. Besides, Dad and I are tapped out in the finance department. It looks like no money for race cars this year."

Mr. Brock smiled. "Samantha, I have what I think is a great idea for you. How about we get together next week for lunch on a day when you're not so busy. My treat."

Sam looked at her favorite teacher and good friend. "Sure, sounds good," she replied. "It will be good to spend some time with you. We haven't had a chance to talk for quite awhile."

Mr. Brock smiled and then he and his wife moved away to give Sam time to talk to potential customers.

For the rest of the day, Sam wondered what Mr. Brock had in mind. *He probably wants to see where I am on the book,* she thought. *I'll take the book along so we can look at it together.*

CHAPTER ELEVEN

Mr. Brock and Sam agreed to meet at a local restaurant for lunch. Sam was suffering from extreme curiosity when they sat down together and ordered. She lay the book down between them.

"Oh, good, you brought the book along. I'm anxious to see where you are in the writing."

Samantha smiled, "I had a lot of time to work on it this winter and I think it's ready for you to take a look and let me know what you think. I'd like to hear your comments, any changes you might suggest, or anything you see that might make it better. I really value your opinion. After all, if it wasn't for you, I probably wouldn't even have had the courage to be doing this."

"That's great Samantha. I can't wait to sit down and go over it carefully. As far as your courage goes, I think you have plenty of that."

Sam said a simple thank you.

After the waitress took their orders, they sat back and looked at each other.

"Well," Mr. Brock began. "I have an idea to get you back on the track."

Sam chuckled. "It has to be a good one because there is just no money to buy one and not time enough to build one for this year. We'll be busy scraping enough business together to get the profits at the shop back to normal."

Mr. Brock was still smiling. "Okay, here's my idea. Are there cars around that you could buy right now?"

"Sure," Sam replied, "As you know, I had moved up to pro stock. There aren't as many of those around for sale but, sure, I could probably find one. But like I told you, no money in the Taylor family for that right now.

"How much for a good pro stock with a good engine?" Mr. Brock asked.

"I would say about ten thousand – five for the chassis and five for the motor, give or take a few hundred. Also, you might find one for sale really cheap from somebody who just wants to get out of it for one reason or another. Maybe they've run out of money or the driver and the rest of the family have just lost interest. You never know; there are a lot of reasons to want to quit the sport."

"Interesting," said Mr. Brock, "I didn't know those things cost that much. There must be more to them than I ever thought there was."

"Oh sure, you invest in a roll cage, wheels and racing tires, beefed up steering, driver's seat, and racing steering wheel, fuel cell, and aluminum high capacity radiator and you have a lot of money tied up in the chassis. Add stuff like gauges, a seatbelt system and a lot more and it all adds up fast."

"Then you send the engine out to be re-worked, buy a new carburetor, and pretty soon you're up to ten grand. And most drivers who build their own cars don't even count the hours they have in the job. You'd probably be looking at another five grand if you included the hours you have put in."

Mr. Brock whistled quietly. "Wow, I had no idea."

"Yep, that's the story and that's why I won't race this year. Next winter I'll build another one myself."

The waitress came and set their sandwiches down in front of them. Sam was hungry and took a big bite out of hers.

Mr. Brock continued to sit back and eyed Sam. "I'm going to loan you enough money to buy a car," he finally blurted out.

Sam was so surprised she almost choked on her sandwich. She coughed, wiped her mouth and put her hands, palms out toward Mr. Brock.

"No, no, no sir," she said, eyes wide open and looking at Mr. Brock. "You can't do that; I won't let you. I just can't take your money."

"Sam, it's a loan; you're going to pay it back."

"Mr. Brock, I can hardly afford a candy bar. I have no savings — nothing. All the extra money I ever had went into racing. My folks don't have anything either. The fire wiped us out. It took all their savings to get up and running again. We hardly get by day to day. How could I ever repay you? There's only money in racing for the top five or six in each class. The rest just barely get by with a couple of good sponsors. Most locals lose money on the whole deal."

"Okay, I understand, but here's my plan. I'll loan you the money and you promise me you'll finish your NASCAR art book. We'll publish it and you can pay me back with the money you make from that. What do you think?"

"I think "no," Mr. Brock. It's a great idea and I sure do appreciate it, but I just can't take your money. Besides, how do we know we can get my book published? If it doesn't happen I can't guarantee you'll ever get your money back. That would make me feel awful. It would make me sick."

"Samantha, listen to me. I have some extra money. You know Mrs. Brock and I both teach. We don't have any kids and we look at you like one of our own. I want to do it. Mrs. Brock is with me on this. Sometimes I think she's more excited about it than I am. Besides, I know your book will be a success. I've shown some your rough drafts to a friend of mine in publishing and he thinks it has promise. NASCAR is big; the fans will eat it up. I don't think there is another book out there like yours. Besides, it's a way I can hold a hammer over your head to make sure you finish it. You've got talent and I want you to use it."

"No, Mr. Brock, I just can't do it. I don't know what else to say."

"Samantha, don't say anything right now. Go home and think it over and we'll talk about it next week. I know your folks will have reservations also and I'd be glad to talk to them, too. You have to understand that I'm very excited about this. We'll have some fun with the whole project."

"Okay, I'll think about it but right now I don't think it's going to happen. But I do want you to know that I sure as heck appreciate your offer."

"Good, let's get together next week and we'll talk some more. You know, I've done a little research and I've been told that you are one of the best drivers in the northeast. Maybe we'll end up in NASCAR — who knows. If that happens, we'll all be rich and famous." He leaned back in the booth and laughed, his face lighting up with pleasure.

Sam joined in the laughter. "Boy, that would be nice, but that's a very long road with a lot of bumps and potholes in it."

"I know, Sam, but it's nice to dream about things like that."

Sam looked at her older friend. He had always been so good to her.

"I can see you're really into this, Mr. Brock, and I really appreciate your interest and your offer. And thanks so much for your help in school. It always meant so much to me."

"You deserved it, Sam. I was happy to help you. I know you well enough to know that you won't disappoint me. Just think about my offer and talk to your folks about it."

Sam smiled at her friend and turned back to her sandwich. "Okay. Thanks, Mr. Brock; I'll think about it, that's for sure."

On her way back to the shop Sam did think a lot about the proposition and how lucky she was to have a friend like Mr. Brock. She also considered how great it would be to get back on the track and race again. She had been worried about missing a whole season.

CHAPTER TWELVE

Sam returned to work after meeting with Mr. Brock. Her dad was curious. "Well, what did Mr. Brock want? You two are always cooking something up."

Sam thought how to best answer her father. "He wants me to finish the book and try to get it published. I gave him my rough draft and he's going to go over it. It's just about done."

"Nothing wrong with that; I certainly agree with him there. Your mother and I think that would be great. Now that racing is out of the picture for this year, maybe you'll have more time for it."

"Well, funny you mention that. He said he would loan me the money to buy a car and I can pay him back from the book sales."

"You're kidding me; he'd do that?"

"Yep, he thinks people today want all kinds of NASCAR stuff and the book will sell. He says he'll be happy just to see the book completed and he's helping me with it."

"Well, what do you think? Are you going to do it?"

"Dad, I'm going to do some serious thinking about it. I'd be taking on a big load. I'm sure I'll have a lot more work to do on the book before I submit it. If it's accepted, the publisher will probably recommend even more changes."

"If you finish that book, you'd really make your mother happy. She just loves your art work. You know, you could just finish the book and forget about racing until maybe next year. I'm sure Mr. Brock would still help you out with it. I know he wants to see you published as much as Mom and I do."

"Yeah, I know, but the racing really appeals to me. It would be hard for me to wait another year knowing that the money is available right now."

"I understand, Sweetie, you really love racing. So do I. I just want you to know that your mother and I can't help you out this year. We've got to get the shop back to a money-making business again. Maybe next year, but this year is out of the question. You'd be on your own with the whole deal."

"I understand, Dad. I'm sure Mr. Brock and I can work it out if I decide to go for it."

"Before you make up your mind, why don't you see if there are any used pro stocks available and how much they want for them? I heard Chuck is quitting. His trucking business is growing like crazy and he doesn't have the time to race. Maybe he'll sell you his car. But you probably know more about that than I do."

"Yeah, Chuck and I have talked about it. He definitely doesn't have the time to race or even work on the car. It's a good idea, but he can't afford to just give me the car. I'll call him this afternoon. Dad, if you and Mom have any more thoughts on this, I'd be glad to hear them anytime."

"Okay, Sam, we'll let you know if we think of anything. Also, if this deal goes through, can you put the shop name on the car and advance me some credit until next year? How about if I pay you for both years next year?"

Sam laughed and put her arm around her father's neck. "Sure, Dad, I'll trust you. Just remember I might need a little extra time now and then to work on the car if I get it."

They both laughed and turned back to their work.

That afternoon Sam called Chuck Turner. "Hey, buddy, I hear you're hanging up your Nomex," she said, referring to the fireproof material that racing suits are made from.

"I'm thinking about it; how did you hear that? I remember telling you that I didn't think I would have time to race, but I don't think I said anything to you about quitting all together. I thought you'd be disappointed that you wouldn't have me to push around on the track anymore."

"Dad told me."

"Oh, yeah. When they get together, my Dad and yours start gabbing and drink so much coffee I don't see how they get to sleep at night."

Sam laughed. "That's for sure. So it's true?"

"Yeah, the business keeps me so busy it's the only thing I've got time for anymore. I was going to keep the car and just put her up on blocks in case I get the time and urge to go race again. Why?"

"Well, I have a new sponsor — a really great one, a dream deal," and she went on to explain the offer from Mr. Brock.

Chuck listened and finally said, "Wow, sweet. Sounds like you want to buy my car."

"That's about it. What do you think? Want to sell?"

"Sam, if it was anybody but you, I'd probably say no. But I know you'd take good care of her and I know how much you want to race. Also, it will give me an excuse to go to the races just to watch you and my car. I know you'll get the best out of her."

"Hey, you can pit for me with Dave when you have time. We'll make a great team."

"Sounds great," Chuck happily replied.

"Now, how about price? How much do you want for that heap that I passed just about every week last season?"

"You mean that heap that you passed when you weren't trying to leap fences to get off the track?"

"Now, now, I had a little help with that, if you remember."

They both laughed.

Chuck turned serious. "I have about thirteen thousand in her, but I want to see you on the track. If you put my business name on for a sponsorship I'll give you a real deal. You and Dave made some really nice changes to it and you can finish that up. If I could I'd give it to you, but I'm tapped out and borrowed to the max on the new truck line. It shouldn't take more than a thousand to finish it and I could use the cash. How about five thousand?"

"Are you sure, Chuck? That sounds like a real good deal."

"Yep, I'm serious. I want to help you as much as I can."

"Thanks, Chuck, sounds like a plan. Let me talk to Brock and I'll get right back to you."

"Okay, buddy, good luck. I'll talk to you as soon as I get home."

"Terrific, have a great day. Are you coming over Sunday? I really miss you."

"I'll try. I miss you too; I could use some hugs. It's been really tough the last few weeks. I'm bone tired and need a break and a good home-cooked meal."

"You come to my place Sunday and you'll see. I'll make you all better. You haven't even seen the new apartment. Dad and I finished it last week and I'm all moved in. I bought some furniture at a second hand store – bed, sofa, and TV. It's not great stuff but I call it home."

"What time?" Chuck asked, "One o'clock okay?

"One will be just fine. I'll be waiting for you. Love you."

"I love you too. See you Sunday."

⁓

Sam was very happy. Everything was falling into place. She broke the news to her father and mother and told them about the excellent deal she had made with Chuck. They were very happy and wished her well and gave her big hugs. "You'll do okay, Sam. Just keep all four wheels on the track; you can't afford a big bust-up."

"That's for sure, Dad. That car is going to have to last the whole season without major repairs. I know the engine is good. Chuck took good care of it and it doesn't have many races on it. He had just replaced it. Also, it's a Jack's Speed Shop engine so you know it's good."

Dave overheard the whole story. He ran over to Sam, picked her up in a big bear hug, and lifted her off her feet. "Yahooo!" he yelled, "we're going racing. I can't wait. This will be an excellent year. When can we get that baby in here to check her out?"

"How about Saturday afternoon? I think Chuck will be home by then," Sam replied.

"You bet, let's get right at it. We need to finish up the conversion to pro stock and that shouldn't take long. All we have left to do is move the engine back two inches. We'll get the seat and steering wheel set up for you. We'll have to repaint with our colors and the lettering will have to be changed. That will be a breeze, no problem. Look out, Fonda, here we come."

She called Mr. Brock that evening who was pleased that Sam had made up her mind and that the deal with Chuck was so good.

"I'll make the check out to you and you can pay Chuck. I'll make it for the original ten thousand because you'll need some extra money to get to the races and finish the rebuild."

"Yeah, I lost my Nomex suit, shoes, and helmet in the fire, which will cost me a few bucks. I don't know how to thank you, Mr. Brock; this is really great."

"You don't have to thank me, Sam; we'll just get going on the book. I had a chance to look it over and I think it looks great. Just a few touchups here and there and you should be ready to submit it."

"Don't worry, I pulled out all my sketches last night and already made some changes. My mom will be right there prodding me along, too. She's all excited about the whole project."

"Good, good. Your mom can keep you going when I'm not around," he said with a laugh. "And you know I'll be around. I'll give you all the help you need, Sam; just call me anytime you get stuck or need advice."

"Okay, Mr. Brock; I'll be working again on it tonight."

"Good; talk to you soon," he replied as he hung up.

Her green eyes blazing, she hung up the phone. Sam was excited. Back on track. *How lucky can I be*, she thought; *life is good*. Sam sat back thinking how lucky she was. She had lost a lot in the fire but new doors had opened. Sam's career dream was back on track.

That night she worked on the book until early in the morning. She was pleased at how nice it was turning out.

Mr. Brock, her mother, and others had finally convinced her that it was a worthwhile project and that she did have great talent for art.

She also called Chuck that night and told him the deal was on; she wanted to pick up the car the next day. "That's cool," Chuck said. "I'll put a charger on the battery so she'll be ready to roll in the morning."

Saturday afternoon came and Sam and Dave drove her truck and trailer over to Chuck's huge storage building where Chuck's car was stored. Chuck met them at the bay where the car was stored on blocks. They were so excited!

When they pulled the dust cover off, the car sat there gleaming as if it had never been raced. Chuck told Sam it had been sitting there waiting for her.

Sam whistled. "Wow, she looks great," she said as she and Dave checked it out.

"Well, let's see how she sounds, "Sam said as she climbed in the driver side window and settled into the seat. Chuck and Dave were laughing again.

"What?" she asked as she pulled herself up and forward so she could see out of the windshield and reach the pedals with her feet.

"Oh, very funny. Yeah, I know, I've got to do a little seat and steering wheel adjustment here," and she started laughing as she clowned and lowered her head even more so she was peering through the steering wheel spokes. "This car doesn't fit someone a foot shorter than the previous driver."

Dave reached in and patted her on the shoulder. "We can fix that, no problem," he said.

She flipped on the switch for the fuel pump and ignition and the starter switch. After two or three coughs and spits the powerful racing engine roared into life. Chuck and

Dave looked in and laughed at Sam's big grin. Two or three of Chuck's workers came running into the garage and they, too, broke out with big grins.

"Yeehaw," one shouted. "Let's go racing!"

Recognizing Sam, he then shouted, "Go get 'em, Sam; can't wait to see you back on the track. Fonda aint been the same without you and Chuck out there. At least one of you will be back." Again he shouted out, "Yeehaw!" over the noise of the engine.

Sam, Dave, and Chuck laughed openly as Sam shut the engine down. The smell of racing oil and fuel filled the area, which added to the happiness. Sam felt the excitement course through her body. Her green eyes glowed and an even bigger smile spread across her face. *Dang, back on the track again,* she thought.

"Ahhh! Smell that?" Chuck said as the room filled with exhaust fumes. "I've been missing that smell. Okay, here's your check back; I'm going back to racing," he joked.

Sam looked at her boyfriend. "Oh no, you're not; you're too busy — remember?"

Sam started the car again and drove it up onto the trailer. They shut the engine off and toggled the car down.

Chuck and Sam gave each other a quick hug and a kiss and Sam climbed into her truck.

"See you tomorrow," she said. "Mom's cooking pot roast just for you." And she blew him a kiss out of the truck window as they headed out of the truck parking area.

Chuck watched with a longing in his eyes. *Wow, these guys are happy. I wish my schedule allowed me to get back in the game.*

Chuck had a plan he had been thinking about for a while. *Maybe we can expand this racing thing for Sam and do some big time NASCAR racing,* he thought as he turned with a wave and went back to his office. He had investigated how much money it would take to run the NASCAR Camping World East series and was eager to try it out. His accountant had put a bug in his ear hinting that it would be better for the business if he spent some more money on advertising — especially to get the new business going in the south.

When he approached his father with the accountant's suggestion his father was very interested. He had told Chuck, "You're the boss now; do what you think is right. I don't understand all this new accounting stuff anyway. In my day you made money and never spent more than you made. Today who knows what these young accounting wizards are up to? It's your baby now, Chuck; go for it."

He explained his plan to his father. "Thanks, Dad; I know we've talked about moving Samantha up into the modified class here but that would only benefit us locally. I'm thinking about buying a car to race on asphalt and run the Camping World East Series."

His father leaned forward behind his big desk and gave Chuck a strong gaze. "Whoa there, fella; you're talking big money now."

"I know, Dad, but think about it. If we race that series it will cover a lot of the territory where we do business; the tracks run from North Carolina to Maine. We can invite customers to watch the races and invite prospects for new business to attend also. I think it would do us a lot of good; hopefully we can pick up some new accounts and some bigger ones we have always wanted up and down the east coast. With the new truck line we took on, we have trucks running most of those routes anyway, so why not get as many clients as we can along there?"

Chuck's father stroked his chin and leaned back in his big office chair. Dan Turner was a big man and every time he leaned back in his chair like this, Chuck winced a little bit, afraid that the chair might break and spill his father out on to the floor. It was Dan's favorite position when he was thinking.

"Do you have any idea of what it would cost?" he asked.

"Dad, I figure we can buy a car and a hauler and meet expenses for less than $200,000. I've already been online and checked out used equipment."

Dan looked at his son. "So you think it's a good investment — that we'll pick up enough new business to cover the expense?"

"I think so. We probably won't break even the first year and if it's too big a loss, we can always quit, sell the equipment and just stay local with Samantha."

"This is probably a silly question, but have you thought about a race team or a driver? I say silly question because I have the feeling that you and Samantha already cooked this up."

"Come on, Dad, no way. I would never think about a move this big without talking to you first. You and I are the only ones who have discussed it. And, yes, I want Sam to drive for us. I think she has a great future in racing. You know as well as I do how good she is."

"Okay, I guess this is something you really want to do and you're willing to assume responsibility if it doesn't work out."

"Absolutely. I just have a fantastic feeling that this is the way to go. I've worked it out with accounting and it would cost us at least half a million if we had to cover that whole territory with TV, radio, and newspapers. Also, you know that many of the decision-makers in the companies we deal with are gearheads and love racing. They'll have a ball in the pits, watching the races, and meeting Samantha in person."

"Okay, obviously you have faith that Samantha can adjust to racing on asphalt."

"No problem, Dad; she's as good as they come. And speaking of Samantha, she's easy on equipment and she's not going to smash up a car just to win on a grudge or anything like that. And Dave knows race cars in and out. He's an excellent tuner and knows how to set up a car so it handles. I'd rather have people I know in charge instead of strangers."

Dan came around the desk and clamped a big hand on his son's shoulder and they shook hands. "Okay, let's do it!" he said. "It looks like you've covered all the bases and I'm looking forward to going to some of those races myself. I'm sure Sam's Mom and Dad would like to join us, too. It'll be fun and I'll get a chance to talk to some customers I haven't talked to for years, except on the phone."

"Thanks, Dad. I really appreciate your faith in me. I won't let you or the company down."

"I'm sure you won't, Son. This company will be all yours one of these days anyway. I know you'll take good care of it."

"I'll run it by Sam and Dave as soon as I work out more of the details."

Dan smiled. "I'd love to be there and see the looks on their faces when you tell them."

"Well, when the time comes to tell them why don't you come with me and we'll tell them together?"

೭ꔸ

It took Chuck a few weeks to work out all the details and arrange the financing for the CW race series; during that time he kept the project a secret from Samantha. It wasn't easy but he wanted her to concentrate on her racing in case the deal for the new car didn't, for some reason, go through.

Once in a while, Sam sensed something was up as Chuck seemed to be lost in thought and a bit distant from her. When she asked if anything was wrong, he always said he was just working too hard and had a lot on his mind. She was happy with that and really never suspected that the next season would change her life dramatically.

CHAPTER THIRTEEN

Sam and Dave worked from sun-up until sun-down to get the car ready to race in the pro stock class. They had moved the engine back the two inches that the rules allowed and installed a nine-inch transmission that Bill Wilson had given her. She was grateful for that as nine-inch transmissions could be expensive. Samantha was grateful for any money she could save on the project. She bought new rims so that she could put bigger tires on the car. She would have liked a crate engine, but that would have taken all the remainder of her cash reserves. *Maybe next year we'll buy a new engine,* she thought, considering the extra power.

It was Saturday — race day. They gassed up the car and loaded all their gear and spare parts into the truck bed. They were ready to go. Sam felt they were as ready as they would ever be when they loaded up to go to the race.

They got to the Fonda track and registered. Sam and Dave were excited. It was the first race with the new car. With the fresh paint it stood out among the other cars. It had no dents, no dirt, and was polished to a high shine. Sam's racing friends all came around to take a look. Sam was glad she had the extra money from Mr. Brock to pay the entry fee and the other expenses for preparing the car. She also had enough to purchase a new Nomex fireproof suit, racing shoes, gloves, and helmet.

She looked great walking around the pits decked out in her new gear — coordinated with their racing colors. She had even outfitted Dave with the team colors and her mom had stitched "Crew Chief" over his left front pocket. Dave wore his new uniform with pride.

The new paint job looked great. It was an eye-catching yellow and blue. Bold letters spelled out "Taylor's Complete Auto Repair" on the door panels and "Turner Trucking" on the rear fenders They had missed the first few races of the season and the annual car show at the local mall, but Sam was just happy to finally be racing again — especially since she was now in the pro stock class.

Sam greeted old friends as they came around to admire her car and say hello. Some had started racing the same time she had and the friendships had grown over the years. She knew, however, that very little of that friendship extended to the track. No driver would ever intentionally hurt another, but there was a fine line between pushing hard and bumping others and straight-out racing. "Rubbin' is racin'" some of the old-timers liked to say and sometimes the rubbin' part got a little rough. A race driver on local tracks had to learn how to take it as well as give it.

"Sam, you did a great job on Chuck's old car. It looks brand new," some said.

Sam joked back, "I'm sure when you jockeys start bumping me out on the track, it won't look quite as new for long," and they all laughed.

Sam knew Chuck was in town and he met them in the pits.

He gave Sam a big hug and kiss and they got to work checking out the car. Much excitement was in the air. A happier pit crew could not be found.

The car had needed very little work. All she had to do was adjust the front end alignment. She had personal experience with the car's inability to hold in the corners so she changed the castor and camber to her liking as well as altered the weights over the rear wheels.

She wouldn't know for sure if the adjustments were correct until she tried it on the track at warm up and practice laps. She would soon find out for sure how accurate their adjustments were.

She and Dave had discussed the new settings. Dave had worked on stock cars just about all his life and he knew how to make them go fast and handle like they were on railroad tracks. He put that experience to work for Sam. Both agreed that something had to be changed, but nobody knew exactly how much change to make and they just guessed at it from watching the car perform when Chuck had driven it. The only thing they knew for sure was that it was just too loose and wild in the corners and it was a big effort to do a controlled skid and hold the car on the track in the corners. That had to be fixed one way or another.

Sam took the car out for practice and told the crew to take a little weight off the outside rear. "Now it's getting too much grip and doesn't want to slide," she told Dave.

Dave and Chuck made the adjustment and took five pounds off the outside right rear. Sam went back out again and declared it perfect after running a couple more practice laps.

Sam came in sixth, missing the fifth position which was the cut-off for qualifying. She was just not that secure in the new car and had backed off a bit. She didn't want to crash in the first race., She only wanted to get some seat time to get used to the car. If she didn't qualify for the main that night she wouldn't feel too bad, even though she wanted to do better. *Everyone will understand if I don't qualify tonight*, she thought.

When she got back into the pits, Chuck and Dave met her and told her she looked great. "How's the handling?" Chuck inquired, "It looked pretty good from here. You didn't seem to be fighting it a whole lot, but we couldn't tell for sure. It looked like pretty smooth sailing."

Sam climbed out of the car with a big smile on her face. "It handled perfect," she said. "It couldn't be any better. Lucky us, we guessed just right. Dave, your experience really made the difference today. You were right on the money. I christen you the Taylor Team handling expert. Nice going, pal."

"How was the power?" Chuck asked.

"Not bad, but I'm not going to able to keep up with the guys with the new engines or the ones who had a lot more money to max out the engine than we did. They're pretty fast. I have to make up the time in the corners. That's where I've got them."

She entered the LCQ (Last Chance Qualifier) and lined up in fifth place for the start. It was not an easy race, as most of her competitors were experienced pro stock drivers who knew all the tricks. They didn't like to get beaten by a "girl" and they blocked her every chance they got. This was everyone's last chance to run the main, so they were ruthless. One driver tried to put her out of the race in the fourth turn, but he wasn't aware of Sam's skill. He pulled up to her on the inside in turn four and tried to push her into the wall. Sam punched the brakes, he passed, and using her cornering skills, she flew by him on the inside. Sam was totally in control as she rocketed by him, completely sideways. She smiled her big "go fast" smile.

Another driver blocked her for almost a full lap. She bumped him a few times from the rear, causing him to go too fast into a corner and losing it as Sam sailed by. She ended up in third place and qualified for the main. She was a very happy young lady.

Dave and Chuck met her at the pit entrance and hitched a ride standing on the side crash bars, hanging onto the windows on either side of the car. Dave was whooping like a kid. He didn't care who heard him. The other pit crews smiled and waved at the happy team as they drove by. Sam gunned the engine with her foot off and on the throttle. It was a sound everyone loved — a sound of victory.

Sam drove into her pit area and shut the car down. She climbed out into the arms of both Dave and Chuck. They took turns hugging her and giving her high fives. She pulled off her helmet and her long dark hair fell over her shoulders, her beautiful green eyes blazing.

"What a car; what a race!" she cried out. "I had some of those guys faked out of their jock straps. Oops," she said and put her hand over her mouth. "Did you see all of that? A couple of them tried to push me right off the track, but I put them away."

"You sure did," Chuck said with his arm around her shoulders."You have become a tiger — and a cool one at that. I'm glad I wasn't out there running against you. I wouldn't stand a chance."

"Oh, you know I would have been easy on you," she said with a sly smile.

"I don't know, you looked pretty tough out there — a lady with a mission! You wouldn't let anyone take your eye off the ball."

"Anything need fixing?" Dave inquired.

"Nope, Mr. A1 pit man; just gas her up. We're going to run the main."

"Yes, ma'am," Dave exclaimed enthusiastically and gave her a mock salute.

She started the main in sixth place and held that pace. She didn't want to push too hard right now as she was not yet that sure of herself in the new car. She was challenged a few times by the cars behind her, but she held them off. She watched one car disappear off the track when he tried to pass her on the outside and still she held her line. He turned into her to try to scare her and they scrubbed side by side. She heard metal against metal and cringed at what she knew was the end of a perfect paint job. She glanced over her shoulder just in time to see him disappear in a big cloud of dust. *He's not going to be happy with me, but these guys have got to learn not to mess with this lady.*

On the sixth lap of the ten-lap race the engine started to heat up. The temp gauge on the dash was right to the limit. She had been watching the gauge very carefully as she didn't want to blow the engine in the very first race. *This baby has got to get me through the races left this year. Right now, I can't afford a new engine.*

The temperature did not get any better as she slowed. She decided to pull into the pits. She knew Dave and Chuck would be disappointed but she wanted to save the car for another day. As she slowed she knew she had made the right decision as steam began to billow out from under the hood. She still worried about serious damage to the engine. *Maybe I should have pulled in earlier,* she thought.

Chuck and Dave jumped on the sides of the car and rode in with her to the pit area.

"Overheating," she yelled to them over the rumble of the engine. Her disappointed crew shook their heads in frustration when they heard her.

They pulled into their pit area and lifted the hood to see that one end of a radiator hose had come loose. They looked at each other and shook their heads.

"One loose screw is all it takes to ruin a race," Dave said, thoroughly dejected. "Sorry about that, Sam, I should have spotted that. I guess I just missed that screw."

Sam raised her hand to Dave. "No problem. Maybe that was just ready to give out. Maybe it needs a new clamp. Who knows? We're not going to sweat the small stuff right now — plenty of time for that. Don't worry about it. I'm really happy." A big smile spread over Sam's face. "Did you see me hang with those guys out there? I know for sure we've got a winning machine here. Next week we'll nail them all to the wall."

❧

And they did. The next week they won the Feature. They had gone over the whole car with a fine-tooth comb the week before and went over it again the night before the race. They were ready and they had no mechanical problems at all. The car ran flawlessly. They gave each other high fives all around in celebration of the win. It was a clean sweep.

Mr. and Mrs. Brock came to all the races and went down to the pits with Samantha's mother and father to congratulate her.

"Boy, Samantha, you really showed them around the track tonight. I'm so proud of you. You really looked great out there," Mr. Brock said.

93

Mrs. Brock was gleaming. "We're so happy for you, dear. What a great race. You made it look so easy."

"I have a great car, you guys, thanks to you."

"Sam, when that book of yours is accepted for publication, you'll be able to pay me back easily. I'm not losing one minute of sleep over it."

Samantha received hugs, kisses on the cheek, and congratulations from her mom and dad.

Chuck Turner joined the group. "Boy, you and Dave have really got that thing dialed in. I don't think it ever ran that strong for me. You made some of those guys look like they were out for a Sunday drive with Mom and the kids. That was a great race — sweet!"

"Thanks, Chuck."

"That's a great engine, Sam. I knew that before I sold the car to you. When I had that thing built, I went all the way. I just couldn't get the chassis tuned in well enough to stay on the track."

Sam laughed. "Yeah, I'm very much aware of that."

A smile broke across Chuck's face. "Yeah, I remember. At least now you know I didn't do it on purpose. That thing was a bear to handle in the turns. I'm glad you and Dave got that problem solved."

Dave, Sam, and Chuck got the car loaded up and made their way to the bleachers to watch the rest of the races with their friends. They all remarked how well Sam's car had run and what a great job she had done driving. It was a great night. Mr. and Mrs. Brock, her mom, and dad joined them and agreed with them.

CHAPTER FOURTEEN

Things were going well at the shop. Many of Sam's friends came in for service and to chat with Sam and take a closer look at the car they loved to watch at the races. Sam pointed out some of the changes she and Dave had installed on the car. They also trusted Sam and knew their heroine would treat them fairly and give them great deals on repairs and parts.

Business was good. Jim and Mary kept a close eye on the business and were very cautious about estimating to be sure they received a fair profit on each job. Their goal was to get the business back to where it was before the fire.

Sam and Dave cared for the new car very carefully. Sam didn't take unnecessary chances during races and Dave kept the car in good running order.

There were some unforeseen and unavoidable problems. One week Sam was pushed into the wall and damaged the right front quarter to the extent that they had to replace the wheel and steering gear on that side. She couldn't finish that race and had to accept a tow back to the pit area.

At another race, a fan belt broke and the time it took to replace it put her into last place.

Another race found them on a very muddy track with worn tires. Sam could not afford a set of new tires that week and quit in the middle of the race because it was just too hard to keep the car on the track. Sam pulled out rather than take a chance on wrecking the car.

Mr. Brock was there, saw what happened, and bought Sam a new set of tires. When Sam protested, Mr. Brock asked her if she was working on the book and making changes that he had suggested. Sam had said she was and Mr. Brock insisted on buying the tires for her.

"Don't worry, Sam. I'll just add it to your bill." he said with a laugh.

Sam laughed, too.

"If that book doesn't get published," she said, "I'll be mowing your lawn and running errands for you for the rest of my life."

CHAPTER FIFTEEN

By the end of the season Chuck was so busy with his trucking business he didn't have time to attend all the races. When he did, he was more and more impressed with Sam's driving skill and Dave's mechanical abilities.

After one of the last races of the season he came to the pits to congratulate Sam. She was especially glad to see him as her mother and father couldn't make it, and Mr. and Mrs. Brock couldn't make it either. Having Chuck there was like having family present.

"You know," he said, "I've been thinking. How would you like to race on asphalt next year?"

Sam looked at her friend with a questioning look. "I'd love it, but that takes a ton of money, a lot more money than I have. Just the travel alone is expensive, to say nothing about buying a new car and a hauler, entry fees, and other expenses I probably haven't even thought of yet. You're talking big money. Why, what did you have in mind?"

"Well, you know the trucking business is growing like crazy. I have the funds to spend some more money on advertising and I might as well do it on something I really enjoy. Local racing just doesn't do it. I want to get the word out all over the east coast. I've been looking online at the Camping World East series. The circuit stretches from South Carolina to New Hampshire, just about matching the area our trucks service."

"That sounds great, Chuck; where do I fit into that picture?"

"You fit in as the driver of the new Turner Trucking Camping World East car."

"Oh yeah, right, Chuck, You're kidding, aren't you? I don't have any experience on asphalt. I thought you were thinking of me for crew chief or something like that. Driver? That's a big gamble on your part. I only know sliding sideways in the dirt. On asphalt, you don't slide sideways unless you're headed for the wall. I don't have the slightest idea how to run on asphalt."

"Come on, Sam. You know your way around any track and you're no dummy. Your reaction time is great, you're not afraid to take some sensible chances, and you and Dave take really good care of your equipment."

"Maybe so, but it would take me a while to get used to it. Those guys move twice as fast as I'm going around a dirt track."

"I'm not worried about that," Chuck replied. "You learn fast; you're a natural. Besides I know and trust you. I know you're not going to ruin a car just to get even with some guy who bumps you. You never did that here and I don't expect you to do it there either. I trust you with our equipment. You'll do the best for us."

"But the expense, Chuck; you're talking big money. Not only big bucks for the car but also a transporter, hiring a crew, motels and restaurants on the road — big, big money. Are you sure you want to do all that?"

"You let me worry about that. I told you business is going great and I need to get the "Turner Trucking" name out there. There are a lot of execs of companies who like car racing. They'll know if they do business with "Turner Trucking" they'll be able to get into the races and can get into the pits when we come to town. That means a lot to them and their families and hopefully they'll send more business our way."

"Wow, I can't think. Let's talk more about it next week. I'll call you and we'll get together for some lunch. If you're serious, I'd be a fool not to say "yes" as long as I can work it out with Dad and you don't need any money. I'm broke most of the time. My race winnings don't even cover expenses."

"I'm serious for sure. I'll call you. Hey, I'll see you for Sunday dinner tomorrow. We can talk more about it then."

Sam smiled. "Great; see you then."

"Okay, see you tomorrow. We have a lot to discuss and you can tell your mom and dad what's going on. I made my dad promise not to tell your folks so you would have a chance to talk to them about it first. But with those two buddies, you never know. Your dad might know about it already."

Sam nodded her head. "Yeah, probably."

"I'll bring my computer over. I have pictures of a car and a hauler saved on it. You're going to love it. It's a pretty cool rig."

The two friends laughed, and then Chuck gathered Sam's small frame in his arms and they kissed. "See you tomorrow," he said as he strolled away.

Sam couldn't wait to get home and talk to her mother and father about the good news. All the way home, Dave kept glancing at her and prying her for details. He had heard the whole conversation between Sam and Chuck and he was excited, too.

"Sam," he nervously asked, "I'd love to be part of the crew. Do you think you could work that out?"

Sam turned quickly to him. "Absolutely, Dave, I wouldn't get in a car unless you were right there. You're my right-hand man. But I don't know anything about racing on asphalt!"

"Good, that makes two of us."

They laughed and joked about it all the way home. Sam's dream appeared to be coming true thanks to Chuck.

Dave sat back and smiled. He was happy with the thoughts of becoming a NASCAR mechanic.

CHAPTER SIXTEEN

Sam and Dave got back late that night and over breakfast the next morning she broke the news to her mother and father. They were both interested and were anxious to learn more.

"It's not 100 percent yet, but it looks good. Chuck is very pleased with the way "Turner Trucking" is going. His business is booming and he wants to do some advertising along the east coast, invite customers and friends to the races we enter and just get the word out about Turner Trucking. The southern addition has really come in as a good money maker for him," Sam told her mom and dad. "He has to work out the details and nail down the actual cost. We don't know exactly how much a car is going to cost. We'll need a tractor/trailer hauler and that's going to cost a lot, too. Then we have to figure out how much it'll cost to go to the races — entry fees, licensing, lodging, and food. There's going to be a lot of things to consider before a final decision."

Her mother gazed at her lovingly. "Oh, Sam, I'm so happy for you. All your dreams are coming true. How lucky you are and what wonderful friends you have. You've worked so hard for this. And now — you're going to be a NASCAR driver. How exciting, I can hardly wait."

Sam and her dad laughed, "Whoa, Mom, not so fast. We're not there yet. A lot of things have to come together. We don't even have a car yet."

"The only thing is I'm so afraid you might get hurt …" Mary's voice faded away.

"Mom, don't worry, I can steer clear of any wrecks most of the time. In all the years I raced Fonda I haven't gotten hurt, except for a very stiff neck for a couple of weeks, thanks to Chuck. I'll be okay, don't worry."

Mary persisted, "But they go so fast at those races — sometimes almost two hundred miles an hour in the cup cars. If you ask me, that's too fast."

"Mom, they have so many safety features today that serious injury doesn't happen very often. The Hans Device head restraint and the safer barriers built into the track walls have changed the racing scene and made a big difference in lowering the injury rate. Besides, at my level we reach top speeds of maybe 100 on the straights. Average laps are less than 100."

Jim was quiet and thoughtful. Finally he said, "sounds like the Turners are really serious about this whole deal and in my experience, if the Turners say they can do it, they'll do it. No problem. In all the years Mom and I have known them they have always been straight shooters and Chuck is just as reliable as his mom and dad. We often talk about how lucky we are to have such wonderful kids. When I think of some of your classmates who have no interests except partying, I am so happy to have you as a daughter. I'm just so proud of you. Besides, I'm looking forward to going to some of the races with you. We can go with the Turners and have a great time. We might just take you, Chuck, and Dave out to dinner once in a while."

Mary perked up a bit and said, "And I'm looking forward to appearing on TV with you just like all those other NASCAR moms and dads that we see."

Sam and Jim sat back in their chairs and chuckled. "Well, Sam, looks like we've got your mother sold on the deal, but I've got to think about the shop also. That means you've got to let me know how much time you'll have to work. I'm sure most of yours and Dave's time will be spent working on the racecar, so I'll probably have to hire one or two people to take your places. I hope you'll work on the car at the shop because having the car and the hauler there should generate a lot more business, especially if you park the transporter out front for all to see. People will want to deal with a shop that supports a NASCAR car. At least I think they will. By the way, I'm glad you're taking care of Dave in this deal. He's a good man."

Sam agreed.

CHAPTER SEVENTEEN

Chuck came for dinner that Sunday. The talk around the dinner table centered on the new sponsorship and asphalt racing. Chuck was excited as he had made some progress toward securing the equipment that would be needed to put a NASCAR race team together.

Chuck was so excited he could hardly sit still in his seat. He was pretty sure he had lined up a car, and a tractor-trailer camper combination to haul it. He grinned as he talked.

"I found a complete package," he said. "This guy is getting out of racing and he wants to sell his whole rig — car, hauler and all. He told me that the engine on the car was refreshed at the end of the season last year and he'd only raced two races with it this year. They went over the whole car inch by inch. If we wanted to replace the engine it would cost about thirty-five grand. He said it's all set up to run the Camping World East series and you could race it right now without doing a thing to it."

Now it was Samantha's turn to smile. "Wow, Chuck, you're moving pretty fast here. When you make up your mind to do something, you don't waste any time, do you? That sounds fantastic. Have you talked to your dad about it? I would never want to do anything like this unless he was completely behind it."

"No problem. He had been thinking about it himself. I think he's looking forward to going to the races. My folks and your folks together at the races will be something, won't it? They'll have a ball. Hopefully they'll treat us poor racers to a nice meal at a great restaurant now and then."

Sam laughed, "Yeah, that'll be cool."

Jim smiled. "Sounds good to me," he exclaimed.

Chuck leaned forward to his girlfriend and winked, "Dad and I have the finances all lined up for the whole project. It's a done deal." He smiled. "I'll be working until I'm ninety-five to pay off the debt, but it'll be worth it."

The two friends high-fived each other.

Now it was Sam's turn to squirm in her seat. "You gotta tell me about the car. I just can't wait any longer."

Chuck got up and brought his briefcase to the table. He set it by his seat and reached down to retrieve his laptop, set it up on the table between them, and opened it up. "The guy sent me pictures of the car this morning. It's sweet — hardly a scratch on it. He said it had never been seriously wrecked. The engine alone is worth more than what he is asking for the whole car. He said he'd sell the car without the hauler for twenty-five grand."

They looked at the pictures and practically drooled over them.

"Wow," is all Sam could say. "Look at her; sure is nice. It's all good stuff on it. I can't believe he'd part with the car for twenty-five."

Chuck leaned towards his friend, "Look at the equipment list. It's got a Muncie T10 transmission, Carrera gas shocks at five hundred bucks a pop, dual ignition, ceramic-coated headers, Halon fire suppression system, and a lot more. Look, it's even got a helmet cooling system for those real hot days.

"His radio system goes with it, too. The helmet is wired and includes two pit crew stations. Along with all this, he said he'd give us some extra tires and wheels, spare parts, and everything else he's got on hand. Put on top of that the value of the engine at thirty-five thousand and it's a real deal."

The two friends poured over the pictures and equipment list. Mary and Jim came around the table and stood behind them. "It just looks too good to be true," Jim said.

Sam leaned back with a smile on her face. "I probably won't be able to sleep tonight thinking about this. It's just a dream come true. You're putting a lot of faith in me, old pal. I hope you know what you're doing."

"Sam, I know what I'm doing. I love racing, too, but now the first thing on my mind has to be the business. You're going to be good for it. People like you, and you are one heck of a driver. I'm proud to have you on the Turner Trucking team. I thank you for coming on board. You and Dave will be good representatives for us."

"Thanks, Chuck. I'm pretty nervous about the whole thing, but you know I'll do my best. Now tell me about the hauler. That sounds great, too."

"Okay, I can pull that up on the computer, also. It looks good. It's a '96 International 4900. It's a complete camper on the back with shower, toilet, 120 gallons of fresh water and a twenty gallon hot water tank. You can take a shower after the race. Dave can drive home while you shower and vice versa."

"It has a full kitchen and refrigerator so now you've eliminated the need for motel and restaurant reservations and the hassle of getting to them. We've got to watch the budget — especially the first year. You'll have everything you need right in your camper, including beds, so you can get lots of rest before and after races. It's even got air-conditioning along with a big diesel generator built in. Now, listen to this — I can get the whole package for about $150, 000."

"Wow; sounds good to me," Sam beamed, "but I'm not the one laying out all the money. I thought we'd be pulling the car on my trailer with my truck. You've thought of everything, Dude."

"Man, we're going first class!" Chuck gave out a very loud "Yahoo!" and jumped up, almost bumping Mary and Jim. He raised his hands over his head in a victorious motion, grabbed Sam around the waist and lifted her off the floor, and gave her a big hug and a kiss. He looked at Mary and Jim and gave them hugs, too. Then he reached into his briefcase and pulled out a bottle of champagne.

"This calls for a toast," he said, and Mary went to the closet for champagne glasses.

They were seldom used and dusty. "Let me just clean these up; I'll be right back." She disappeared into the kitchen.

They turned back to look at the pictures.

Chuck looked into Sam's sparkling green eyes. She was looking at him with rapt attention. It seemed every time he looked at her closely he was taken away by her beauty. He marveled at how someone so little and so pretty could be so strong and have such great talent for racing automobiles. He had the feeling she could race just about any vehicle — stock cars, motorcycles, sports cars, Indy cars, whatever, and do it well. *I'm so lucky to have her as my girl,* he thought.

"By the way," he said, "it's a stacker trailer so we can get two cars in if we get to the point where we need a spare. Meanwhile, maybe you'll want to take a car with you so you and Dave will have something to run around with if you need it.

"We'll park it at your shop so people will see it and want to come in to look at it. It'll be a draw for new customers. It's a good thing you put in that oversized bay in the new garage. You can do the re-painting and decals there over the winter."

Sam saluted. "Taylor's Auto Service is ready to help you, sir. That'll be one job that I'll really, really enjoy."

"Chuck, I trust the guy you're dealing with. He sounds like a straight shooter, but I would like to have Jack look over the engine this winter. I just want to make sure everything is okay. Dave and I can pull the engine or just take the car over as soon as we get it and Jack can take a look at it."

"That sounds good to me. I agree. We can't be too sure. It would be a bummer to get all the way out to the first race and then find out something is wrong during practice. I'd like to hear Jack's opinion on the engine, too. I'm sure he might have a suggestion or two on how to make it run a little stronger if we need it. Maybe not, but I'd like him to look at it anyway. Let's get off to a good start."

"Okay, when can we pick up the rig?" Sam said as she rubbed her hands together.

"How about next weekend? We'll drive out, load my car into the trailer, and drive the whole unit back. It'll be a little test run for the hauler. It's only to Syracuse, so that's not a big deal. We should get out and back on Saturday with no problem. I'll just pick up a cashier's check at the bank and we'll be on our way. I'll call the guy first and tell him the deal is on and to expect us."

Sam jumped up and hugged her boyfriend tightly.

"Okay, I'll be ready; what time?"

"How's six a.m.?"

"Fine with me," she said, so excited she was almost jumping off the floor.

"Sam, I want to run the whole series if we can, so mark March 27th on your calendar."

"What's that?"

"The first race in Greenville, South Carolina. Also, if you don't mind, I'll put Dave on my payroll so he can feel free to work on the car and rig whenever it needs it. He can help you out when he's not working on our stuff. That way your dad can hire someone to take his place."

"Chuck, I don't know what to say. I'm just flabbergasted. This is all happening so fast. I didn't really think you were so committed to this. Wow! You are putting a lot of faith in me. I hope I can live up to it."

"Sweetheart, I've been thinking about this for quite a long time. I've done all the numbers and discussed it with Dad. We both agree that the advertising value is well worth it. Besides, it'll be a hoot. My mom and dad are looking forward to going to the races with your folks. They'll have a ball. I'm looking forward to some really fun times. It'll be exciting."

"Geez, I hope I don't let you guys down."

"Sam, you just keep it on the track and you'll do fine. We'll make sure you've got the horsepower and the handling. If we just make it near the top ten next year, I'll be happy. The second season we should have all the bugs worked out and then we'll start thinking about moving into the top ten — and maybe more."

"Well, here's another adventure for two kids who started racing at Fonda all those years ago." He hugged Samantha again. "I can't tell you how excited I am. Tomorrow, I'll make some calls and check out licensing and whatever else we have to do. I'll also have my lawyer draw up a contract for us. I don't want you running off to another race team if you become really successful next year."

Sam laughed. "Chuck, you sure don't have to worry about that. I just hope I can get the hang of asphalt racing quickly and can produce for you."

"You'll produce or I'll jump in that thing and drive it myself, and you don't want that. You're twice the driver I ever was. You're going to be a star, Sam."

Sam laughed. "I guess we'll find that out pretty quick, won't we?"

CHAPTER EIGHTEEN

Over breakfast the next morning, Sam and her parents discussed her obligation to talk to the Brocks about the new plan.

"I'm sure Mr. Brock will work with me on this. I'm almost done with the book. All I have to do is let Mr. Brock edit it and make any changes he recommends and we'll send it out to the guy he knows in publishing. I can always sell Chuck's car and give that money back to him. I don't want to do that right away because I still want to be able to race at Fonda now and then as the Camping World series schedule allows. That series is only ten races this year so I'll have plenty of open weekends to race at Fonda."

"Well, dear, you'll just have to work all that out with the Brocks. Like you said, you can always sell your pro stock car. But if the book is published, maybe your worries will be over. You can repay the Brocks with that money."

"Sounds good to me," her father added. "You're in pretty good shape now, thanks to Chuck."

Sam turned to her mother. "Mom, remember that chat we had last fall when I was so depressed? You said that if I concentrated on all the good stuff in my life miracles might happen. Looks like you were right." She gave her mother a hug.

Jim was puzzled and looked at the two of them. "What's this all about?"

Mary winked at him and said, "Oh nothing, dear; just girl talk."

Sam called the Brocks and told them she had some big news and they agreed to meet her at their favorite lunch spot.

∾

After greeting each other and sitting down at the restaurant, Mr. Brock opened the conversation. "Well, you certainly got our attention, Sam. We can't wait to hear the big news."

She smiled. "Well, here it is," she said. "Chuck's business is growing faster than he expected and his accountant says he needs to spend more money on advertising."

Mr. Brock smiled. "Well, that's good news. I like Chuck. He's a very nice person and a hard worker and I'm happy to see him get ahead in the world; but how does this involve us, or you, other than being his girlfriend, of course?"

Sam decided to come right out with it. "He's going to put together a NASCAR team and he wants me to be his driver."

Mr. Brock leaned back in the booth and whistled quietly. "Wow," he said, "business must be really good. I've been doing a lot of research on car racing lately and I know Cup Car racing means really big bucks. He must be doing really, really well."

"It's not as expensive as you think, Mr. Brock. It is much more expensive than racing locally, but there is more than one level of NASCAR racing. At the top are the Cup Cars, and then the Nationwide series. Chuck wants to run in the Camping World East series, which is the next level down. He wants to run that series because the schedule is run on racetracks that almost mirror the area where he does business, from Maine in the north down to South Carolina. It's good exposure for Turner Trucking and he can entertain customers at the races. He's very excited about it and has already lined up a car and a transporter to haul our car and all our gear that we'll need to race."

Mr. and Mrs. Brock beamed at their young friend. Mrs. Brock said, "We are so happy for you. You look positively gorgeous; success looks good on you."

Sam's face reddened at the compliment. "Thanks, Mrs. Brock. It does feel great. And I can't thank you two enough. You've stood behind me and that means a lot to me. I'll never forget that."

Mr. Brock smiled, "My pleasure," he said. "But what does that mean for the car we just invested in? Does that mean we won't be able to see you race locally anymore?"

"That's one of the things that I want to talk to you about. I'd like to keep my pro stock car to race locally when the schedule permits. The asphalt series is only ten races and I'd like to continue racing Fonda if it's okay with you. Also, the book is almost done so I was wondering if you could help me edit it and then send it to your friend in publishing. Hopefully, it will bring in enough money to pay you back the money I owe you."

"Sam, that's great and you keep the car. You've kept your end of the bargain by finishing the book and we definitely want to see you race locally. Maybe we can travel to some of the Camping World series to see you race there. That would be great, too."

"Okay, it's a deal. You guys are terrific. I don't know how I would have gotten by without you. Wait until you see the equipment Chuck bought for us! And I can't wait to see the book published. That'll be wonderful, too."

They finished their lunch and waved goodbye to Sam as she pulled away in her truck.

Sam couldn't wait to get back to the shop and tell Dave and her family what a beautiful day it was for her. All her dreams were coming true.

CHAPTER NINETEEN

At 6:00 a.m. Saturday morning, as promised, Chuck pulled up to Taylor's and jumped out of his red Corvette that he loved so much. With the first profits of the now-successful trucking firm, he finally bought the car that he'd admired at the local Chevy dealer's garage.

He had piled quite a few miles on his beautiful Corvette driving to North Carolina and back each week. After 30,000 miles the car still sparkled like new.

He called up to Sam's apartment.

"You ready, Miss NASCAR?"

"Be right down," she replied; "just getting a jacket."

Sam bounded down the stairs and turned her face up to Chuck to receive a quick good morning kiss.

"Okay, Chucky baby, let's go get the new stuff."

Chuck opened the door for her and she slid into the car. It was one of the things she loved about him —the little courtesies he extended to her. She was a sturdy, strong, and competent race car driver, but she was also a girlfriend and she loved Chuck dearly.

On the way to Syracuse, they chatted about the next season. Samantha had had a tough week and was tired and fell in and out of sleep.

"You don't mind if I sleep, do you, Chuck? If you get tired, you can just wake me up and I'll do some of the driving."

Chuck looked over at her and smiled. 'Hey, you don't think I'm going to let a woman drive my Corvette, do you? I'm not too sure you can handle it."

Samantha smiled and closed her eyes. "That could possibly be funny if I hadn't crossed the finish line ahead of you so many times over the years."

"You were just lucky," he said with a laugh.

Samantha smiled and closed her eyes. "Yeah, right."

She fell into a deep sleep as the little coupe ate up the miles. She awoke as they pulled off the interstate at the Syracuse exit.

Chuck had set the on-star satellite global positioning system with the address of their destination and pulled into the driveway of the Gutowskis — the people who had the rig for sale.

Bob Gutowski came out to greet them and shook hands with them both. Chuck introduced Samantha to Bob.

"Nice to meet you," he said. "I've heard a lot about you."

Sam smiled; "I hope it was all good."

"Oh, yes. I can't wait to see you on a track — hopefully in this car."

Sam spotted the new rig right away and was pleased at what she saw. The truck, camper, and trailer were polished and looked brand new. The shiny well-cared for racecar sat behind it, waiting to be loaded.

Bob followed her gaze. "Well, what do you think?" he asked.

Samantha looked at him and all she could say was, "Wow! You sure have taken really good care of everything; it all looks brand new."

"Yeah, my son and I have always taken good care of all of our equipment. We hate to see it go. You're going to love the car. We have all the setup notes for all the tracks in the CW series. By the way, Chuck told me a little about your skills. You're going to be the driver, right? If you're as good as he says you are, you should be in the top ten in no time at all."

"Yep, I'm the one. Top ten? I don't know about that. I'll feel great if I just get through the first lap at the first race. Can we start her up?"

"Sure can; I've had the oil heater on all morning and she should start right up. Hop in."

Sam climbed in and Bob and Chuck laughed as Sam's eyes barely came to the bottom of the driver side window."

"Another six-footer drove this last, right?" and she laughed along with them. "We can fix that."

She flipped the switches and the engine roared to life immediately. She had a huge grin as she gunned the engine.

"Beautiful," she said as she shut the car down and climbed out. "That engine sounds sweet and runs great. If you took as good care of the engine as you did everything else, we should be very happy with it."

Chuck stood in the background and smiled. "Well," he said, "I can see you like it alright; you want to buy it?"

"It's your money, boyfriend; if you're happy, so am I."

Bob nodded his head. "I know you won't be sorry. This was my son's project. He's getting married and racing just doesn't fit into his calendar now. He's not here because he couldn't stand to see it go down the road. He's sick about the sale. Especially since he got into the top ten last year and came close to winning two of the races in the series. Samantha, you're going to love this car. It'll take some time to get used to racing on asphalt, but when you get used to it, you can be sure you've got a car as good as anyone else's out there. Also, we'll help you out. I'll come to a couple of the first races and I'm sure my son, Stan, will want to come, too. Between us, we have about forty years of experience with racing on asphalt. I know we can help you. We'll get you going real nice, no problem."

Sam nodded her head. "That's real nice of you, Mr. Gutowski. I sure can use all the brain power I can get. I'd love to spend time with both of you to get your advice. I would like you to talk to my mechanic, too. He's a real whiz at dirt track racing, but like Chuck and me, we're babes in the woods when it comes to asphalt."

"Give him a few days and then give him a call. He loves to talk about racing. I know he'll want to come to the races with me and I'm sure he'll want to help you out."

Sam and chuck checked out the hauler, camper, and trailer. Bob and his son, Stan, had loaded all the spare parts in the hauler and he showed them where everything was stored, explained all the different spring rates, and showed them the four extra shock absorbers.

Sam was impressed. "I'll never learn to utilize all this stuff. You've got to be a high tech wizard to figure this all out."

Bob smiled. "If you think this is a lot of technical stuff, wait until you start dealing with tire pressure, tire wear, castor and camber, weight bias, track bar settings, and how all these settings affect one another."

Samantha shook her head. "Oh boy, don't tell me anymore, I won't sleep for a week. I thought we could just change the decals on the car and the trailer and go racing. Luckily, I'll have all winter to get up to speed on all this stuff. Besides, my mechanic is a real smart guy and he's had a lot of experience."

Bob nodded. "That's great," he said; "A good driver doesn't mean much without a good team in the pits. I hope I can be there when you race."

Sam laughed. "Don't come to the first race, it'll probably be a real mess and very embarrassing. We'll get the hang of it eventually. I'm so glad you took such careful notes. That will give us a place to start and we can go from there."

Bob went to a large cabinet in the front of the trailer and opened a door. "Here's a little surprise for you. Look at it as a bonus. I forgot to tell you this went with the deal."

Chuck and Samantha's eyes lit up as they looked in at a brand new engine in a crate.

Bob saw their eyes light up and held up a hand. "Don't get too excited," he said; "this engine is brand new, but it's totally stock. You'll have to do a lot of work on it to get it anywhere near the one that's in the car already. With some work at least you'll have a spare."

Samantha grinned, "We have just the right guy who can build engines with the best of them. He's built a lot of engines for Chuck and me over the years. He'll have that up to maximum ponies by next spring."

Chuck shook Bob's hand and thanked him. "This is very nice of you," he said, "and we won't forget this."

Sam and Chuck checked out the truck, camper, and trailer and then loaded the two cars in and toggled them down.

Chuck handed Bob the check and they said their good-byes. They were soon back on the road, this time in a huge hauler rig.

Chuck took the wheel, as he had a lot of experience driving trucks for his Dad when he was growing up. He made a lot of short hauls with trailer trucks as well as straight trucks, doing deliveries in his spare time when he was in high school. Upon graduation, he went to work for his father and started to learn the office. He eventually ran the office and now the whole business as his father stepped further and further into retirement.

Samantha was always eager to learn anything new and she watched carefully as Chuck went through the gears in the big truck. "If you're not loaded with that much weight, you can start out in second or third gear. Also, get used to shifting without the clutch. Clutches are expensive and if you shift carefully you don't need to use it except when you're starting out from a parked position. All you have to do is get the engine rpms equal to the transmission and you can shift easily. It'll take some time to get used to it, but a gearhead like you will catch on in a hurry.

"Notice that my first shift was about one-half way through the first intersection. You don't want to over rev a diesel engine. This is a ten-speed trans. Some of the bigger rigs have thirteen speeds. This is pretty light duty for this truck. This engine could haul a lot more than what we're pulling here.

"Basically what you have is just like two five-speed sports car transmissions. You go through the gears once, and then switch to a higher range by hitting this switch on the gear shift and go through the gears again. In high range first becomes sixth, second becomes seventh, and so forth.

Of course, we're not hauling that much so you can occasionally skip a gear shifting up or down, but that takes some experience."

Sam watched as Chuck maneuvered through the streets to get back on the interstate. She was anxious to get behind the wheel and try out the big rig.

Chuck noticed her interest and said, "Hey, let's get a bite to eat at a rest stop and then you can drive a ways. How's that?"

"Sure, why not; I've got to learn how to drive this thing eventually."

"By the way, I can arrange for you and Dave to get a CDL trailer truck license through the business so you can spell each other on long trips."

"Good idea, Hon. I'm so lucky to have such a smart boy-friend," she said with a sly smile.

He laughed. "Yeah, and just think, if the racing thing doesn't work out you and Dave can come drive trucks for me."

"That crack is going to cost you, buddy," Sam shot back.

"Sorry, honey, only kidding," Chuck said realizing he had carried the teasing a little too far. Every once in a while he forgot how serious and dedicated she was to her racing career.

After their meal, they returned to the truck. "Hey," Chuck said, "let's try out the beds in this thing. I could use a little nap."

Sam grinned at him. "No way," she said. If I'm going to be driving trucks for you, I'm going to have to prove to you that I won't have to take a nap at every rest area."

"Oh, come on."

"Nope; I told you that crack was going to cost you. Paybacks are tough, you know. I'd take a hug and a kiss, though. Besides we told the folks we'd be back before dark."

He let out a big sigh. "Okay," he said reluctantly, loosening his hug. "Let's go. This will be your first driver's lesson."

Samantha climbed up into the driver's seat, adjusted it to her liking, started the engine, and pulled out of the parking area. She shifted flawlessly up through the gears and checked her mirrors when they hit the entrance to the interstate.

Sam never ceased to amaze him. She drove the rig as if she had been driving for years. He instructed her on how to pass slower traffic and at first she hung back, but soon was passing with no problem. Chuck told her how to use the rear view mirrors to make sure she didn't pull back into the driving lane too soon and chance cutting off the passed vehicle.

A couple of faster rigs went by, noticed the pretty driver at the wheel and beeped their horns as if welcoming Samantha into their tribe.

She had her big go-fast grin on her face as she realized she had reached and passed another milestone in her life.

Chuck looked over at her and laughed at her grin. "Is there anything you can't do?" he said with pride.

She glanced back at him. "Haven't found it yet, Sweetie," and she laughed loudly.

CHAPTER TWENTY

When they pulled into the shop, they saw a lot of cars parked there even though it was Saturday evening.

"Oh, oh, something's up," Sam said. "I think a party might be happening here."

No sooner had the hiss of the air brakes quieted then they looked out and saw a whole group of their friends come running out to greet them.

Chuck looked at Samantha. "I think your folks have been on the phone since you called them. Looks like a full-blown party to me."

Sam smiled at Chuck, "I think you might be right," she said and they climbed down out of the cab amid camera flashes and loud cheering.

"Come on, give us a tour of the new racer chaser," someone called out.

Jim Taylor hugged the two of them and said, "Forget the hauler; I want to see that race car."

Samantha held her hands up to them. "Okay, okay," she said with a laugh; "give us some room to unload."

They raised the door to the trailer and everyone tried to look in at once. Chuck got to the Corvette, untoggled it, got in and slowly backed it out.

When Sam was sure Chuck was clear, she pushed the buttons to lower her new race car down to the trailer floor. As the low slung shiny car came into view, cheers and admiring ooh's and aah's broke out among much clapping and cheers.

Dave came up to Samantha and gave her a big hug. "Wow, Sam, beautiful. I can't wait to get my hands on her."

"Wait until you hear her, Dave; she is so smooth."

Sam climbed into the car, shouting out to everyone that she had to be careful as the finely-tuned racing engine was cold and she didn't want to race the engine too much and take a chance on damaging it.

She hit the switches and the engine roared to life. After it warmed up a bit, she did stab the throttle cautiously a couple of times. She revved it up so everyone could hear how nice it sounded.

She shut it down. Most of the men gathered around the car. The hood was lifted and the engine admired. Others checked the interior, the gauges, and all the equipment that goes into a modern NASCAR racer. Samantha answered all their questions and pointed to all the features of the car. The number one question concerned the horsepower. "How much?" they wanted to know and Sam answered casually — "about 800."

The answer came easily to her lips each time, but each time a little lump moved higher in her throat. *I'm going to be driving an 800 horsepower car?* she thought. *That's a little different from the 600 I'm used to.*

The women headed for the camper and Chuck showed them all of its great features. Everyone was pleased with the new addition.

Gradually the crowd thinned as the picnickers headed for home. The only ones left were Jim and Mary Taylor, Chuck's mom and dad, Dave, and the Brocks. Jim and Mary and the Turners were beaming with pride as they gazed at Sam, Chuck, and the new race car.

Mrs. Brock broke the silence. "How exciting, I can't wait until next spring to see you in the new car."

Samantha looked lovingly at the little group.

"Yep," she said with a smile and some tears, "next year is going to be exciting and I owe it all to my mom and dad and all my wonderful friends right here with me." She moved to Chuck's side and put an arm around him. "Of course, Chuck had a little to do with it, too. I'm going to be doing my best to make it a happy and successful year for all of us."

CHARLIE LOOMIS

Follow Samantha's exploits in the new book, *Stock Car Sam Races NASCAR*.